T0346855

WHAT FEASTS
AT NIGHT

WHAT FEASTS AT NIGHT

T. KINGFISHER

TITAN BOOKS

What Feasts at Night
Trade edition ISBN: 9781803369686
Broken Binding edition ISBN: 9781835410585
E-book edition ISBN: 9781803369693

Published by Titan Books
A division of Titan Publishing Group Ltd.
144 Southwark Street, London, SE1 0UP
www.titanbooks.com

First edition: February 2024
10 9 8 7 6 5 4 3 2 1

A CIP catalogue record for this title is available from the British Library.

Printed and bound by CPI Group (UK) Ltd in Croydon, CR0 4YY.

This one's for the War Flamingos.

WHAT FEASTS
AT NIGHT

1

A poet once wrote that the woods of Gallacia are as deep and dark as God's sorrow, and while I am usually skeptical of poets, I feel this one may have been onto something. Certainly the stretch of my homeland that I found myself riding through was as deep and dark as something out of a fairy tale.

Autumn was nearly spent, which meant that many of the trees had lost their leaves. You might think that would mean that the woods had opened up, but if you think that, you have likely never been to Gallacia. Serrated ranks of pine lined the road, with the bare branches of oaks thrusting out between them like arthritic fingers. The sky was the color of a lead slug and seemed barely higher than the trees themselves. Combined with the wagon ruts that left a ridge down the center of the road, I had the unpleasant feeling that I was riding straight down a giant throat.

Everything was damp. Water dripped from the trees, and the fallen leaves had formed a slick brown mush that coated the ground like cheap gravy. Only the evergreens retained their elegance. If this was a fairy tale, it was the kind where everyone gets eaten as a cautionary tale about straying into the woods, not the sentimental kind that ends with a wedding and the words, "And if they have not since died, they are living there still."

The road sloped upward and the trees on the right-hand side thinned out, to be replaced by a high stone cliff. This is normal. Gallacia is, above all, compact. Our cliffs are very high and usually directly on the road, the trees crowd close on all sides, and while we do have more than our fair share of small waterfalls breaking quaintly over mossy boulders, if you try to step back to admire one from a distance, you're likely to fall off a different cliff and break your neck.

Also there are bears.

"You know," I said to Angus, "we *could* still be in Paris right now."

Angus grunted. He was my batman in the war, and now served as a combination valet, groom, and voice of reason. I inherited him from my father, along with my chin, my hair color, and my cast-iron liver.

"I didn't force you to come," he said.

"You blackmailed me."

"I most certainly did not."

"There was guilt. I distinctly remember guilt being involved."

He grunted again. Angus's mustache is sometimes capable of its own independent expressions, and was currently expressing its disdain for my complaints. "I, at least, remember what we owe Miss Potter."

"Believe me, I haven't forgotten." Miss Potter, that redoubtable British mycologist, had more or less saved the world from the monstrosity lurking in the Ushers' lake. An American doctor and I had done a lot of the heavy lifting, but without Eugenia, we would probably still be sitting in the house and wondering why we had started growing strange white filaments out of our ears.

(It had been long enough now that I could joke about it, but only just.)

"I could hardly let her stay in your hunting lodge without a translator," Angus added. "She doesn't speak Gallacian."

No one speaks Gallacian if they can avoid it. Our language is as complicated and miserable as everything else in this country. I couldn't fault Angus's logic. And there was no reason *not* to use the hunting lodge. I had inherited it years ago, and certainly no one else was using it. Still . . .

"Tell me the truth, Angus. Is this a romantic getaway I sense?"

Angus's mustache gave me a quelling glare. "I have nothing but the highest respect for Miss Potter," said the rest of Angus stiffly.

"As do we all. The one doesn't preclude the other, you know."

My oldest and dearest friend muttered something that I didn't quite catch, and let his horse drop back so that I couldn't needle him any longer.

Honestly, it was hard to imagine a *less* romantic setting than Gallacia in autumn. I edged Hob away from the side of the road, where a tangle of vines draped over a bare tree like spilled entrails. The road swallowed another hill and we started down it. I stared between my horse's ears and felt generally ill-used.

Paris, when we left, had been in full glory. Much is made of springtime there, but for my money, a warm autumn is just as spectacular and you don't trip over nearly as many poets. The window boxes of red geraniums glow like embers, and if it rains, it only makes the sunlight glitter more beautifully off the windowpanes.

Not a week earlier, I had been leaning on the windowsill, the smell of fresh bread wafting up from the bakery below my apartment, listening to the sound of two coachmen fighting over a fare. They had called each other the most extraordinary names, but because they were screaming in French, it sounded like a declaration of love delivered in the heat of a grand passion. Truly, Paris was the city of my heart.

And now I was here, back in Gallacia. The country of my birth, such as it was. Riding down a road that made me feel as if I was being swallowed whole.

We started up another rise. Hob, my horse, sighed as only a disaffected horse can sigh. I patted his neck. Hob was an old trooper, but technically so was I and I didn't enjoy it either. "Don't worry, boy. There'll be a nice hot mash at the end for you." I hoped there would be, anyway. I'd written to Codrin, the man who kept up the hunting lodge, to tell him that we were coming. He hadn't written back. I was hoping that it was just because Codrin had never been terribly easy with his letters, but between the grim gray road and the grim gray trees and the grim gray sky—not to mention the profound lack of Paris—I was starting to feel distinctly worried.

"Don't sulk," said Angus.

"I'm not sulking." I didn't want to admit to baseless anxiety, so I added, "It's my tinnitus." This was true, so far as it went. Changes in altitude always set it off, and the train from Paris to the capital had been nothing but altitude changes. I lost most of the trip to a high-pitched whine somewhere inside my head.

Still, it could have been much worse. According to the doctor who told me the name of that ringing in my ears, a few hundred years ago they thought that it was caused by wind getting trapped in your ears. They used to treat it by drilling a hole in your skull to suck the trapped wind out. Now they just said, "Can't help you, sorry," and prescribed laudanum to help you sleep.

Laudanum sounded lovely about now. Maybe that would make the growing knot in the pit of my stomach go away.

There's nothing wrong, I told myself. *You're just tired and cross. Codrin's letter is probably sitting somewhere in Paris, having just missed us. You know what the mail's like here, once you get out of the capital.*

This was all true and it still didn't make me feel any better. Hob clearly sensed my anxiety, but was either too well-mannered or too tired from the trip to make anything out of it.

We'd left the capital behind about five hours ago—me with a splitting headache, Angus with his usual unflappable calm, the horses with the deep suspicion that most horses feel about train rides. Angus had collected the horses, arranged for our luggage to be delivered separately, and we set out immediately. (The greatest city in Gallacia is fine, I suppose, but I didn't feel the need to linger. Imagine if an architect wanted to re-create Budapest, but on a shoestring budget and without any of the convenient flat bits. While fighting wolves.)

The devouring road began not long after we left the city. We traveled from smell to smell, the road rising up into the scent of pines and down into woodsmoke and damp, then back up to the pines again. The smell of woodsmoke usually preceded a small village built in the Gallacian style, the houses clay-plastered wattle, all sporting weathered wooden shingles. Since our local clays are mostly gray, this means that our villages are mostly gray as well. (For a short period after the war, we had lost so many young men that our male population was also gray, which led to the popular tragic song "Silver, Clay, and Frost" that every musician played for about a decade, until we were all heartily sick of it.)

When we finally reached the road leading to the lodge, I nearly missed it. The edges had become overgrown and the potholes were deep enough to lose a sheep in. I turned Hob's head toward it and his ears flicked skeptically. Was I sure about this? Really?

In truth, I wasn't sure. The anxiety in my gut was starting to acquire the metallic taste of fear. *Which is ridiculous. It's an overgrown road, not enemy soldiers coming over the ridge. Get hold of yourself.*

"I could swear that I was paying Codrin to keep this place up," I muttered as Hob began to pick his way along the narrow road. Frost-killed weeds choked the edges. "I send money back twice a year."

"Codrin's older than I am," said Angus, which told me very little since I still don't know how old Angus is. (My guess is late fifties, early sixties, but that was also my guess a decade ago, so I can't be certain. His hair used to be red and is now silver, but that's the only concession he has made to age.)

"Still. He should have been able to hire a few village lads to come hack this stuff down." I paused for a moment, trying to do math in my head. "Err . . . we *do* have village lads now, right? All the ones that were being born back when I signed up? Nobody conscripted them?"

Angus shrugged as if to indicate that the life trajectories of the local village lads was no business of his. Hob sighed again.

"All right," I said, nudging him forward. "Let's go see how bad it is."

*

It could have been worse. That's about the best I can say for it. The lodge was old and had been built to last, so the roof hadn't fallen in and the timbers were still sound. But the door stuck, and I had to jam my shoulder into it to get it to open. The smell of dust and old mouse nests hit me like a living thing, and it was very cold.

It was dark inside. The thickness of the lodge walls meant the narrow windows were already in deep shadow, and all the shutters were drawn. I doubt the windows would have let much light in anyway, given the grime. I lit a match and waved it around, unpleasantly reminded of the Usher mansion and the unlit halls.

Nothing horrible jumped out at me, so that was good. "Codrin?" I called. "Codrin, you here?"

No answer.

"This is a bit much," I muttered. Maybe having a hot meal waiting was too much to ask, fine, but not even a fire?

I immediately felt guilty. Codrin had always been relentlessly conscientious. If he hadn't prepared for our arrival, he must have had a damn good reason.

There was wood stacked by the fireplace. Angus knelt on the hearth and built the kind of cautious, tiny fire that you make when you aren't sure if the chimney is full of bird nests. I blundered around, relying more on my memory of the floorplan than the feeble light of the match. Unfortunately, my memory proved to be extremely fallible, and I banged my shins, my shoulder, and my knuckles before finally locating the kitchen and a set of candles.

Light didn't help all that much. It was a hunting lodge, as I said, which meant that there were dozens of racks of antlers hung on the walls. Cobwebs hung between them like garlands. A stuffed boar's head was mounted over the fireplace, and the less said about that, the better.

Armed with a candle, my first target was the little room where Codrin normally slept. I didn't smell death, but that didn't mean something hadn't happened to him. If he was injured or had suffered a fall, he might be in desperate straits.

The door was open. His window was unshuttered, but a thin film of grime obscured the glass. I stood in the doorway, taking in the scene—unmade bed with sheets spilling off, stand and basin, whitewashed walls with a crucifix hanging over the head of the bed. Shadows leapt as the candle flame moved, and I had a brief, intense sensation that someone was lying curled up under the crumpled sheets. I stepped forward and yanked them away from the bed, half angry at myself, then felt foolish when they slid onto the floor, leaving only the bare mattress behind.

No Codrin.

I felt, I confess, a pang of relief at that. I would much rather that he had left than that he had died in the house. Death no longer shocks me, but I still prefer that it not visit my friends and acquaintances in my presence.

The basin was empty, as was the ewer. No trace of water. The razor on the stand was starting to rust. The candle on the stand had burned most of the way down. A dead moth, wings half burned away, lay entombed in the pool of wax. I got down on my hands and knees and pulled the chamber pot from under the bed. Dry, though with a coating of foulness on the bottom.

"Codrin's been gone for a while," I told Angus, returning. "A couple of weeks at least, I think."

Angus grunted and got to his feet. "I'll go into the village and get us some provisions," he said. "And ask around."

I nodded. "I'll see to the horses." Angus would do a better job of getting information out of the locals. My headache was improving, but I wasn't feeling up to prolonged conversation or, God forbid, haggling.

The stables were in decent shape. No leaks, no rot, and the hay had gone dry and musty rather than damp and moldy. I vaguely recalled that Codrin had kept a donkey and a little dogcart for going into the village, but neither were in evidence. Presumably he'd taken them with him whenever he'd left. On the other side of the stable wall, firewood had been split and stacked up to the roof.

I unsaddled Hob and Angus's gray, led them both into stalls, and picked up the water bucket. A stream ran about a hundred yards from the lodge, but the springhouse was much closer, so I trudged up the hillside toward the entrance.

Gallacia has natural springs the way that dogs have fleas, and they are frequently similarly inconvenient. There are plenty of roads that have odd little sideways curves and jogs to avoid a seep, which would otherwise turn it into a mud pit. Still, they're useful for keeping things cold in summer. You find a good spring, slap a springhouse over it, and then the water runs into deep stone tanks in the floor, which stay cold enough to keep your milk fresh and your butter unmelted.

Our particular spring emerged partway up a hill, which meant that the springhouse was built into the side of it. The low doorway was framed with heavy stones, which made the whole affair look rather like one of those old barrows where the Irish buried their dead kings.

The water channel appeared to be working, but mud squelched under my feet as I approached. I stifled a groan. The overflow from the spring is supposed to run down the channel and into the stream, but of course this, too, was in disrepair. Peering inside, I saw that rocks had fallen down from the ceiling and dead leaves had piled up in the corners. The whole building stank of mildew and wet. The spring water was still trickling from the back wall and splitting into the two stone troughs that ran down either side of the springhouse, but one trough was dry, and the other half was clogged with leaves and had overflowed. Mushrooms grew from the central floor, their thin flesh-colored stems clotted with wet earth. I shuddered. *Fleshy stems, thin white threads growing through the staring eye of a hare . . .*

I forced the memory down. It was just a clump of mushrooms. Hell, it was probably a good thing. *Miss Potter will have something to paint while she's here.*

It looked like a stone had fallen in from the ceiling and blocked off the right side. That was a bit more of a task than

I felt like tackling right now, so I settled for crouching down and scraping mud and wet leaves out of the channel, which was even less appealing than it sounds.

I was bent over, hands full of muck, when my tinnitus came roaring in, a buzzing that rose to the familiar whine, and suddenly I *knew* that the enemy was coming up behind me, my back so exposed that I might as well have been wearing a sign that said INSERT BULLET HERE and I was supposed to be scouting but I'd missed them somehow and I was going to get shot by a Bulgarian soldier and I couldn't even blame them because we shouldn't have been fighting the goddamn Bulgarians to begin with, they were our *allies*, for Christ's sake, we shouldn't even *be* here, and I snatched up the bucket and spun around, striking out at . . .

Nothing.

I stood for a moment, unable to even hear my own breathing through the whine, and then I sagged against the doorframe of the springhouse, the bucket handle dropping from my fingers.

Soldier's heart, my American friend Denton called it. He had been a combat medic during his country's civil war, and he had plenty of experience with it. Mine is pretty mild, all things considered. I know soldiers who can't share a bed with another person for fear they'll strike out in their sleep. (Me, I just don't like having someone else steal the covers.) Usually it's not so bad. Every now and then, there'll be a sound or a smell, or I'll see something out of the corner of my eye, and for a few seconds I'll slip into the war again.

Slowly my tinnitus passed. I took a deep breath and then another, then straightened up, embarrassed, even though there hadn't been anyone around to see me. It was probably the damn mushrooms that set me off. Soldier's heart doesn't know the difference between terrible things. Fungus or cannon fire, it's all just the war.

The water in the channel was a tea-colored trickle. I took my bucket and slogged down to the stream to get clean water for Hob.

God, it was so *quiet*. Somehow I hadn't noticed that before.

Not that there was anything odd about that. I'd come directly from Paris. Of course the countryside was going to seem quiet afterward. "Famous for it," I said out loud, just to hear myself talk. "Peace and quiet. People pay good money for it."

The silence didn't feel peaceful. It felt *thick*. Like the layer of fuzz on your tongue after a hard night of drinking, which you can't see or touch but you can damn well taste. There weren't even any birds singing. (Not that I could blame them, since it was the sort of gray day when even sunlight looks dingy.)

"I'm being ridiculous," I said, still out loud. I dipped the bucket into the stream, and kicked a rock with my boot just to hear the *click-click-plop* of it rattling past the other rocks and into the water.

The image of the unmade bed kept nagging at me as I walked back to the stable. Codrin was exactly the sort of meticulous, responsible person that you wanted as a caretaker. He would never cut a corner, never leave a job half-done. And while I had no personal knowledge of the matter, I would have sworn by the Blessed Mother that he made his bed every morning, too.

"If he got too old and retired, he'd still have made his bed," I told Hob, delivering his water. "Not to mention that he would have sent me a letter telling me that he was retiring, and probably recommending someone for the job."

Hob nosed my shoulder, which I chose to take as agreement.

"Even if he was out in the woods and keeled over suddenly, he'd have made his bed that morning."

I moved firewood into the house. The interior was just as quiet as the woods, if not more so. Which, again, was perfectly normal, and there was absolutely no reason that it should feel as though my thoughts were echoing in the silence. Angus would have told me that it was the emptiness in my skull making them echo. I wished Angus was here.

Christ's blood, he'd been gone for less than two hours. What was wrong with me? It was just an empty house. Shadows lay thick in the corners, but surely no thicker than they lay anywhere else.

I built up the fire, recklessly using up my newly hauled firewood. The shadows retreated, but not far enough. Cobwebs hung thick as rags, and the shadows hid behind them. Orange light licked the eyes of the hunting trophies on the walls—those that had eyes at all. Most of them were simply mounted skulls. The others hailed from the days when the art of taxidermy was not quite so advanced as it is now.

Perhaps it was the trophies that were so upsetting. I have seen that expression in particularly debauched absinthe drinkers, but you hate to see it on a deer.

One of the skulls rolled its eyes at me.

I was against the opposite wall, heart pounding and spine digging into the plaster, before I quite realized what had happened. I stared up at the skull, the empty eye sockets dark as grief. Had I imagined it? Would it be better or worse if I had?

A white moth climbed out of the eye socket. I sagged against the wall and made a noise that could have passed for a laugh if you didn't examine it closely. The moth fluttered away from the skull, settled for a moment on an antler, then launched itself at one of the windows and began to batter itself against the glass.

"Right," I said out loud. My voice tasted strange in my throat. I caught the moth in my cupped hands and went back outside. It fluttered against my palms in a delicate panic, and I released it into the cold gray air.

If anything, the silence outside had thickened. I started to whistle, just to keep from going out of my head. When I glanced down at my hands, they were streaked with silvery dust where the moth's wings had touched.

I could have gone back inside, but instead I pulled out Hob's brushes and gave him a quick brush-down. He leaned into the brush, whuffling, and then gave me a betrayed look when I stopped too soon.

"I have other work to do, buddy."

Hob expressed skepticism that this work could be as important as brushing a very good horse who had been traveling for *ages*.

"I know. I'll be back. I just have to make sure that we have somewhere to sleep and that the mattresses haven't been eaten by mice."

The silence of the woods was disquieting, but the silence of a horse that feels that he has been deprived of his due tribute is eloquent. I retreated to the lodge, feeling distinctly told off, and shut the door against both of them.

2

The upper floor of the lodge was taken up by three bedrooms. I had slept in the largest one the last time I was here, but with Miss Potter coming, it seemed polite to leave it for her, and take one of the smaller ones.

Although unless we clean this place up, I can hardly imagine hosting Miss Potter at all. Granted, she probably wouldn't say anything critical. Miss Potter belonged to a fine old school of courtesy, and if she thought you were doing your best, you could offer her skinned mice and boiled newt-water for tea, and she would by God drink the newt-water with her pinky finger extended and praise the plating of the mice.

Still, it was the principle of the thing.

The mattresses were blessedly free of rodents. I was going to have to lug everything outside for airing, but it was getting on toward evening and a damp Gallacian night was hardly ideal for such a task. I settled for unshuttering the windows and shaking the blankets a few times, rousing a cloud of dust.

I could hardly believe how much the place had deteriorated. It hadn't been like this last time, surely? Granted, that had been . . . err . . .

"Goddammit," I muttered to myself, wrestling a quilt as if it were an enemy. "It hasn't been that long. I'm sure of it."

The problem was that while I had always had an image in my head of the hunting lodge, I was starting to suspect that it had been fixed in childhood and perhaps not updated regularly since. My father bought the place years back and while nearly everything got sold after he died, I'd wound up inheriting the lodge. (Technically, as a sworn soldier, the entire estate was left to me, as my father'd had no sons. This includes the house I grew up in, but my mother actually owns that, no matter whose name is on the paperwork. The lodge, though, is mine.)

I just hadn't spent much time here as an adult. I'd been busy. There had been a war. Several wars. And then a few other things that weren't *technically* wars but involved a lot of soldiers cleaning up messes.

The last time I had been out here was after that godawful mess with the Serbs and the Bulgarians. We'd come in expecting to be helping the Bulgarians fight off the Turks—again—and then it turned out we were shooting at them instead. That would have been bad enough, but my people had been attached to a Serbian unit as scouts. Unfortunately, the commander—

may he shit pinecones in hell—heard *light cavalry scouts* and fixated on the word *cavalry*, which meant that he expected my people to reenact the Charge of the goddamn Light Brigade while his men provided cover fire. *And* their goddamn fancy modern rifles didn't work worth a damn, with the end result that some good people didn't live to see our ignominious defeat. (That commander took a bullet himself near the end, which is the reason I'm out here telling you this and not in a stockade somewhere for assaulting a superior officer.)

I spent most of the following January in the hunting lodge, staring out at the snow. Angus put me in front of a window, otherwise I might have just stared at the wall. It had been pretty bad.

It had also apparently been a decade ago. Christ's blood.

The front door slammed. I came down the stairs to find Angus taking off his riding gloves. "Codrin's dead," he said bluntly.

I'd been half expecting it ever since I saw the unmade bed, but it still felt like a punch in the gut anyway. I couldn't pretend that I knew Codrin well or that we were bosom companions, but I'd known him for twenty years. He had kept bringing me tea while I was staring at the snow. Days' and weeks' worth of tea. The fighting had only lasted two weeks, and I spent nearly twice that staring at the snow, drinking tea. Had I ever thanked him for that?

"Shit," I said, leaning against the wall. "How long ago?"

"About two months." I'd already built up the fire, but Angus poked it a few times until it was arranged to his satisfaction. "He didn't die here." He glanced at me under his bushy eyebrows, and I nodded. It wouldn't have bothered me if he had, but it's still a good thing to know. "His daughter came and fetched him home."

I swallowed a few times. "What got him?" It didn't matter, really, but at the same time, it mattered *very very much*, if you understand what I mean.

Angus shook his head. "Nobody knew, or most likely, nobody would tell me. If they didn't actually know, I'd have gotten ten different stories."

I looked up sharply at that. "Won't *tell* you? Why not?"

"That's the question, isn't it?" Angus sat back on his heels and began unloading his pack, setting out bread and cheese and a bottle of wine that was, fortunately, not from Gallacia. (You really don't want to drink our wine. We export it because we don't want to drink it either.)

"It can't have been something scandalous. Not with Codrin."

"Mmm." Angus found a toasting fork and impaled a helpless slice of bread.

I recognized that as his "thinking" grunt. I grabbed the bucket and fetched water from the stream for us to wash up.

The path from the house to the stream was well-worn under the scattering of soggy leaves. If it snowed while we were here, I was going to have to shovel it if I didn't get the springhouse in decent shape again. Maybe tomorrow I'd clear the rest of the muck out and make sure there were no fragments of mushroom in the troughs.

It wouldn't be the first time I'd shoveled snow here. My vigil at the window had ended when we got nearly a foot dumped on us overnight. Codrin started to clear it, and Angus told me in an undertone that I was not going to let a man forty years my senior shovel the stableyard while I sat on my arse. I took a shovel and Angus and I cleared the stableyard, and then the next day I tended the horses, and after that I started splitting firewood. Then it was a week later and leave was over and I went back to my routine and things were fine.

Well, maybe not fine, but as good as they were likely to get.

Shadows were drawing in thick by the time I was done hauling water. I returned to the main room of the lodge and flopped down in a chair. Angus slid cheese and toast across the table to me.

"If it's a scandal, either it's not a juicy one or they aren't talking to outsiders," said Angus.

I swallowed my mouthful of cheese and washed it down with the wine, which was mediocre by most standards and thus head and shoulders above any of our native wines. "Are you an outsider, though?"

"By local standards, yes." Angus leaned back in his chair, clearly brooding. "Given a few more hours, I could find the town gossip or buy some drinks for a few old campaigners, and probably get the details. Though it's probably nothing."

"Consumption?" I glanced involuntarily toward the door of Codrin's bedroom. "They don't want to mention it, in case we decide it's catching?"

"Could be. Though I'd have sworn that one of the people I talked to was the sort who would gleefully tell you about how their uncle's cousin's second wife's brother sneezed on a day just like this, and then his leg fell off."

I pushed the remains of the toast away. "I'll have to go into town tomorrow to give his daughter my condolences." *Noblesse oblige* and all that, even if I had comparatively little of the *noblesse*.

Angus nodded. "I'll go with you. Need to find someone to come work here. Otherwise we'll be stuck eating your cooking."

"Heaven forfend." I am skilled at preparing exactly two meals: handful of dry stuff pulled from saddlebags, and burnt thing on a stick. It would have been a violation of both hospitality and common decency to offer either to Miss Potter.

"An older woman, ideally," Angus said. "For propriety."

I must have looked blank, because he said, "Miss Potter is English."

I must have looked even blanker, because he added, "Unmarried women shouldn't stay in a house full of men without a chaperone."

"I'm not exactly a man," I protested.

"As far as English propriety is concerned, a sworn soldier is not a respectable guardian of virtue."

"Well, they've got me there," I said philosophically. "Respectable I am not."

(The English have no sworn soldiers, so far as I know. Hardly anyone does, outside of Gallacia.)

"A respectable older woman it is," I said. "But wouldn't *she* need a chaperone if *we're* here?"

Angus gave me a look that said I was being dense.

"Before you go . . ." Angus leaned down and pulled a small amber bottle out of his pack. He didn't even need to open it before I recognized the smell of livrit, our beloved national paint thinner, made from lichen, cloudberries, and spite. No Gallacian soldier would be without a bottle, in case we ever need to remember what we're fighting for. (Mostly the opportunity to be somewhere that has better liquor.)

"Ah," I said. "Of course." I downed the last of my wine and held out my mug. He poured me a single shot worth, then did the same for himself.

"To Codrin."

"To Codrin."

*

Sleep was not kind to me that night. I fell asleep easily—rarely a problem for me, and certainly not after a long journey—but when I woke, the silence lay over the house like a snowdrift. I lay in bed, unmoving, straining my ears for any sound other than my own breathing. I would even have welcomed the squeak of a mouse or the sound of Angus snoring.

But there was nothing.

"I've been in Paris too long," I muttered out loud, throwing my voice against the wall of silence and hearing the words rattle down like pebbles. The contrast made it even worse. Anyway, I didn't actually believe it. If anything, I hadn't been in Paris long enough. After the horrors I had recently experienced in the Ruravian countryside, I really wanted to swear off rural life altogether. I had enough money saved up that I could probably find a decent little place in the city and devote my life to tranquil debauchery.

No matter where in Paris I settled, it would never, ever be this quiet. I pulled the blanket up to my chin and felt very small, like a mouse myself, listening while something huge walked overhead.

3

In the morning, Angus and I rode out to the nearby village. The weather was still soggy and unpleasant, the road still swallowed us down like a cold gray snake, and now there was fog to go along with it. I was in a sour mood and knew it and was doing my best not to take it out on Angus or Hob.

It occurs to me that you may think that I am making a great deal of nothing about traveling, granted that I had spent much of my youth gallivanting across Europe, sometimes while being shot at. Possibly you're right. All I can say in my defense is that while I was in the army, no matter where we went, we had a routine. We got up, we ate bad food, we complained, we tended the horses, we were extremely bored, we ate again, we went to sleep. Occasionally we would go somewhere else and be bored there. Once in a very great while, we would spend an absolutely nerve-wracking few hours, and afterward we would be shaky and bored, but in general, the routine reigned supreme.

When I got out of the military a few years back, the lack of routine was the hardest part. People kept doing things at any hour of the day or night! And expecting me to do the same! I don't know how anyone stands it. Eventually I built a new routine, but it was centered around Paris. I ate at the same café every day, at the same hour, and went to the same public house when it opened, and on Wednesday there was always a salon, which I duly attended, and on Friday there would be a party, and on Sunday, I woke to the sound of cathedral bells and thought "I could go to church," and then I wouldn't. (This was also a vital part of the routine.)

It's not that I object to travel. Normally I like it. I don't even object to Gallacia that much. But after the incident with the Ushers, I had been clinging very tightly to my routine and was almost starting to feel normal again, and now I was entirely upended.

The mist hung thickly over the woods and only receded a little when we reached open fields. We were practically in the town before we actually saw it, as if it had been hiding behind a door hoping that we'd go away.

The town was called *Wolf's Ear* in Gallacian. It was a medium-sized village of about two hundred people, but, like many such towns, the population had shrunk in recent years, so there were more houses than were needed, and many toward the edges had fallen into disrepair or outright ruin. It had two main streets that crossed each other at a sharp angle, with the church fitted into the triangle at the junction and the stone walls of the lichyard angling out between the streets.

Angus took the horses and turned toward the inn in hopes of finding out who might be available to work at the lodge. I shoved my hands in my pockets and went looking for someone who could direct me to Codrin's daughter's house.

Wolf's Ear was not exactly a teeming metropolis, and the chill in the air meant that it took me a few minutes to find someone who was outside. Everyone's shutters were closed against the damp. (Most of the wooden shutters had carved turnips on them. No, I don't know why, it's just a thing we do in Gallacia. In Switzerland, they carve flowers on the shutters, but nobody ever asks *them* why. We just like turnips, okay?)

Eventually I found an elderly man puttering in the front yard of a house. He had quite a good putter going on, picking up one thing, ambling a few feet, setting it down, digging for a minute, pulling a few weeds, ambling on to the next thing. I almost hated to interrupt.

"Good day to you," I called. He looked around, then ambled in my direction, an expression of good-natured interest on his face.

"The Devil overlook you, sir," he said, which is a greeting you don't hear much anymore. I smiled involuntarily.

"I don't mean to bother you," I said, "but do you know where I might find the daughter of a man named Codrin?"

"Codrin?" His smile fell away. "Oh. He's dead, you know."

"I heard, yes. I was hoping to speak to his daughter. Do you know where she lives?"

"Oh, aye." He gave me a long, almost pitying look, then pointed across the road and down the street. "Turn the corner and go down four houses. The one with the blue door, aye?"

I thanked him. I expected him to return to his puttering, but when I reached the corner and glanced back, he was still watching me, although the mist was thick enough that I could no longer make out his expression.

I gazed at Codrin's daughter's front door with sinking dread. *Paying one's condolences* sounds well and good in theory, but in practice you have to walk up to a stranger and effectively say, "Ah, yes, that person you loved so much? Remember how they died horribly? So sorry about that." It's different when it's at a funeral and fresh in their minds, but two months later? I felt ghoulish.

But not doing it would have been incredibly rude, and it wasn't as if Codrin's daughter wasn't going to hear that her father's former employer was back at the lodge. I gritted my teeth and knocked.

The door opened a moment later, and a lean, haggard woman looked down at me. She didn't look much like Codrin, except for her height, but there was something around the eyes . . . I cleared my throat. "Pardon me, but are you Meriam?"

She looked me warily up and down and said, "I am, yes."

I took off my hat and held it in front of my chest. "I'm Alex Easton. Uh . . ." I drew a sudden blank and fell back on polite ritual. "How are you today?"

Codrin's daughter tilted her head slightly and said, "I'm keeping."

"Right," I said. "Of course." *I'm keeping* is what we say in Gallacia to any such inquiry, and it covers such a broad range as to convey no information whatsoever. It can mean "I am filled with unspeakable joy, my gout is cured, and angels attend my every step," or it can mean "a bear just ripped my leg off and I am, at this moment, bleeding out, but please don't make a fuss." Either way, you're keeping.

"Can I help you?"

I took a deep breath and clenched the brim of my hat in nervous fingers. "I heard about your father. Codrin. I came to . . ." *Express my condolences* suddenly seemed absurdly stilted. "To tell you how sorry I am. I just found out, you see."

Meriam was probably twenty years my senior and had deep lines etched around her mouth. The lines deepened as she looked at me. "You're the one who sends the letters." Her accent was pure rural Gallacian, every consonant snapped out like a gunshot.

"Err," I said. "Yes."

A hint of hostility crept into her eyes. "Wondering why I didn't write to tell you, were you?"

"No?" I hadn't been, at least not until she said something. "I didn't . . . that is . . ." I squeezed the brim of my hat with my hands. It occurred to me, belatedly, that she might be expecting me to demand Codrin's last packet of wages back. The thought had never crossed my mind, and if it had, I would have chased it out with my pistol in one hand and a horsewhip in the other.

"I just wanted to tell you that I was sorry," I said. "He was a good man. I hope it was . . . at the end, I mean . . . that it wasn't . . ." Oh God, what are you supposed to say to civilians in moments like this? *I hope he died easy* was true, but you aren't allowed to just *say* things like that.

The lines in Meriam's face grew even sharper. I couldn't blame her. I wanted to jam my hat in my mouth to stop myself talking.

Instead I blurted out, "He made me tea."

Bafflement crossed her face, briefly chasing out the hostility. I took a deep breath, decided that I was committed, and said, "A few years back, when I came to stay. I was wounded." (True, although not in the sense that she probably took it.) "I, er, couldn't do much for a bit. He kept bringing me tea. It was always hot. No matter how long I sat there, he never let it go cold. He must have had the kettle on for eighteen hours straight. It was—kind."

The last word came out strangled. I didn't expect that. I don't cry any longer. I've lost the trick of it. Lots of soldiers do, eventually, and only the lucky ones get it back. But even if I can't, my throat still closes up sometimes, and it closed up now, because I knew I couldn't explain what it had meant, when I sat there staring at the snow for a month straight with my mouth full of ashes and my head full of dead men, that the tea was always there and always hot.

Meriam gazed at me for a little while longer, and then she leaned her cheek against the doorframe. "He used to make me tea when I was sick," she said quietly. "I had pneumonia as a child. The doctor said that cold liquids would make me cough, so he never let it get cold."

I nodded jerkily.

We stood in awkward silence, her in the doorway and me a step down, mauling my hat with nervous fingers. I cleared my throat. "I just came here to say how sorry I was. And that we'll miss him at the lodge. That's all."

She flapped a hand in the air, which may have meant "thank you for your condolences" or maybe "thank you for not asking about the last payment" or, more likely, "thank you so much for bringing up such a painful subject." "Da loved that place. Wanted to die there, I think."

"I'm sorry he didn't get to. No, wait." My hat was never going to be the same, as badly as I was twisting it. "I *mean*, I wouldn't have minded if he had. Errr, obviously I would have minded very much that he had died, but not that it was *there . . .*"

At this point, I managed to wrestle back control of my tongue and cram it back behind my teeth before I could say anything even worse.

Meriam studied me, her eyes tired. "I meant to write you," she said, as if I hadn't been babbling like a fool. "Da told me to. But I've never been easy with my letters, and then he died and with everything . . ." A vague gesture, which I understood well enough.

I was preparing to take my leave of the good woman and label this a successful giving of condolences, when the question that had been haunting me broke loose like a dog slipping its leash.

"Can I ask how he died?"

Meriam's eyes went as cold as chips of flint. I cursed myself for having not just abandoned tact but set it ablaze. "I . . . err . . ." I stammered. "I didn't mean . . . I just . . ."

"Inflammation of the lungs," she snapped, biting off each word as if it were a curse. "That's *all* it was."

The door slammed in my face with a crack like a gunshot. I stood for a moment, clutching the mangled remains of my hat, then went slowly back down the road, toward the church. The putterer had gone inside, but I saw the curtains twitch back as if someone behind them was watching me go.

4

"Did you find her house?" asked Angus when I met up with him a few minutes later.

"Found her house, her, and had one of the most painfully awkward conversations of my adult life." What had Meriam meant by *That's* all *it was?* Had she thought I was going to accuse her of hastening Codrin's death along?

I shook myself. Grief does strange things to people, and there isn't always a logical explanation. "Did you find someone to get the lodge into shape?"

Angus rubbed the back of his neck. "It's the damnedest thing," he muttered. "No one wanted to take it. Before the harvest, aye, I could see that, but there's little enough work going begging now, and still they were turning me down."

"Great." I sighed heavily. I wasn't looking forward to cleaning the lodge myself. It's not that I mind hard work—I don't necessarily *enjoy* it, but I'm not *afraid* of it—but I've no idea how one cleans half the things in a house. How does one black a grate, for example? And would Miss Potter even care if our grates weren't properly blackened? And what in heaven's name were we going to do about English propriety? "So you couldn't find anyone?"

"I didn't say that. I found someone, but you're not going to like her."

My eyebrows went up at that. "Angus, you wound me. I like everybody." I paused, considering several superior officers of days past. "Well, nearly everybody."

"Don't I know it," said Angus, in a tone that indicated that this was quite a trial for him. "Still, you won't like *her*. But keep a civil tongue in your head, because she's quite literally the only person in the village who would take the job."

"Huh. Have we done something to make the locals dislike us?" I wouldn't have thought we were here often enough for that, but perhaps that was a reason in and of itself. Had they been expecting me to return to the lodge like the lord of the manor?

Angus grimaced. "Not exactly. I spoke to a couple of people, though, and there's a rumor that Codrin's illness was caused by a moroi."

"A what?"

His mustache looked exasperated. "You know. From the old stories. The mare, the hag, the old woman that lives behind the woodpile?"

I shrugged helplessly. "Sorry. Not one that I've ever heard."

"Mmmm. No, I suppose not. Your mother never wanted your father to tell the old stories to you children. Said it would give you nightmares. A bit ironic, in the case of the moroi, since nightmares are what they're supposed to bring."

I hunched my shoulders. It was starting to drizzle, which was putting the cap on an already difficult day. "Mother had progressive ideas about education." (This was true. She believed that girls should be educated the same as boys, which was extremely helpful to me in its way. When I swore on as a soldier, I had forgotten just as much geometry and Latin as anyone else in my unit, and I once won a bar bet by reciting the prologue of the *Canterbury Tales* in Middle English.)

Angus grunted. This particular grunt indicated that he thought my mother was a bit barmy, but he was not going to insult her to my face. This is a complex concept to express in a single grunt, but Angus had been with me since I was fourteen, with a shiny new set of pronouns and a rifle I had no idea how to fire.

"You think people won't take the job because they're afraid of this moroi creature?" I asked.

"It's as good an explanation as any."

I worked it over in my mind as we went back to the horses. "Angus, that's a *terrible* explanation."

"Is it?"

"We stand on the threshold of the twentieth century, and people are turning down jobs because they're afraid of a . . . a . . ."

"Hag that sits on your chest and steals your breath," said

Angus helpfully. "And maybe the rest of the world is on the threshold of the twentieth century, but we're in Gallacia, if you hadn't noticed." He frowned at me. "And you of all people should know that we don't always know what we should be afraid of."

"Yes, but . . ." I trailed off. He was right. At the Usher house, I'd seen things and hadn't had the wit to fear them until much too late. But still, a fairy-tale woman that sits on your chest? Really?

I rubbed my hands over my face and thought longingly of Paris.

＊

The Widow Botezatu arrived the next day. She had knuckles like old mortar shells and a nose with a sharp red tip. She had agreed to "do for us" at the lodge while we stayed, cooking, cleaning, and keeping house, and she brought her grandson along in the bargain. He was a large, amiable young man who chopped firewood and milked goats and lifted heavy objects with one hand. When you talked to Bors for very long, you realized that he was slow, and if I had meant *stupid* I would have said that instead. Bors had a mind like a lava flow. It took a long time to get where it was going, but there was no stopping it. I quite liked him.

As Angus had predicted, I did not particularly like the Widow, but that was neither here nor there, because I understood her perfectly well. She needed the money and was grateful to have it and resented both the need and the gratitude. She dealt with that resentment by taking it out on her employer, namely me. Not in her work, of course—it would have been a mortal sin, in the Widow's world, to shirk her duty. So the food was good, if unimaginative, and the boards were worn thin with scrubbing. Meanwhile she bristled and argued if I made any suggestions, and if I went so far as to express a preference, she would gaze at the ceiling and tell God in no uncertain terms what she thought of young wastrels who treated the world as if it were an orchard ripe for plucking and how someday we would learn the truth, to our sorrow.

I had suffered far worse at the hands of drill instructors. I smiled vacuously through these impromptu sermons and slipped Bors extra coins.

Whatever her flaws, the Widow was good at cleaning things, and even better at organizing other people's cleaning. Angus and I scrubbed what she told us to scrub and carried things outside to air and pulled cobwebs off the antlers and dusted the boar head and the dissipated deer over the fireplace. Though our work was never up to her standards, it was at least good enough to be getting on with, as my mother used to say.

I won't swear that my reasons were entirely altruistic. Thumping mattresses and banging grates helped drive back the silence. I could still feel it around me, filling up the corners like some strange auditory dust, but as long as I was moving and making noise and talking to other people, it wasn't able to settle.

Cleaning Codrin's room felt strange. We had to do it, because the Widow certainly wasn't going to sleep on the couch or out in the stable, but it still wasn't a pleasant chore. If you have ever dealt with the possessions of the dead, you probably know what I mean. You take things away and leave behind emptiness, and everything you remove—every sheet and pillowcase, every lost sock and old razor—erases a little bit of the dead person's footprint in the world. You picture your own home being carted away, piece by piece, hopefully by loved ones and not by strangers.

I tried to express this to Angus, who snorted and said, "Don't worry, it'll take ten men to clear your apartment in Paris, and the next tenants will be finding bottles of livrit stashed in odd corners for years." Strangely enough, that made me feel better about the whole thing.

With the help of Bors, we tackled the springhouse again. Even Bors proved unable to move the fallen rock that had blockaded the right side. (I would be lying if I said that I didn't find this just slightly gratifying, since I hadn't been able to budge the thing an inch.) Angus speculated that it had been one of the rocks that made up the ceiling when the springhouse was first built. Luckily, it didn't seem to be load-bearing. Since it wasn't high summer and we had no need of two cooling troughs, we settled for scrubbing out the free side, dredging up buckets of muck and rotten leaves and dumping them out on the hillside.

In deference to Miss Potter's incipient arrival, I left a single clump of mushrooms on the central earthen floor, but asked Bors to rake the rest of them out. Their stems had acquired a whitish crust but the caps were fleshy reddish bulbs. They looked obscene and I didn't particularly want to touch them, but Bors dealt with them with a few strokes of the rake.

Fortunately, once they'd been cleared all that remained was mossy dirt, blotched in places with mold or mineral deposits or whatever specific substance stains the dirt in springhouses.

"Does that look like a person on their side to you?" I asked, pointing to the large stain.

Angus cocked his head. "Looks like a sheep on crutches, if you ask me."

I turned my head sideways and was able to see Angus's sheep, albeit poorly. "Hmm. Bors, what do you think this looks like?"

Bors studied the mossy ground for some time. "Old dirt," he said finally, and went back to cleaning.

By the day of Miss Potter's arrival, the windows gleamed, the chimney no longer smoked, the beds were neatly made up, and the house smelled of fresh-baked bread instead of mice.

"I don't know any of that fancy English cooking," the Widow informed me. "Good country fare is all I do."

I contemplated what I knew of English cooking and fought back a mild shudder. "Your cooking is delightful, and I prefer it to anything that they might serve in London."

The Widow eyed me narrowly, clearly suspicious that I might be mocking her. I gave her my most open smile. "Wastrel," she muttered at the ceiling, but I don't think her heart was in it.

Angus left early to meet Miss Potter at the capital. I offered to come along and was immediately shot down.

"But Angus, it's really no trouble—"

His mustache quivered. "No need to put yourself out."

"But I—"

"No need to put yourself out," he repeated, in the tones of one prepared to pronounce blood feud on an entire family, down to the smallest baby in the cradle.

"Ah," I said. Very belatedly, it occurred to me that Angus might rather like to have five hours alone with Miss Potter. (Apparently a horse was a suitable chaperone, but I wasn't? However that worked?) "Well. Have a fine ride, then. We'll look for you this evening."

He acknowledged this with a head dip and a mustache twitch, and was gone.

I decided to make myself useful by going out after game. This was a hunting lodge, after all, and while I had never actually done any hunting here, what with one thing and another, surely there had to be something edible in the area. My father had done some hunting here before I was born, though I didn't know how successful he'd been. Roe deer didn't seem too unlikely, though. Presumably there were also larger deer, but if I actually got one, I would have to carry it back, and that seemed excessively ambitious.

"Watch for bear," said the Widow, as I came down the stairs.

"I will."

"And boar." She frowned at my rifle. *"That* won't stop a boar."

"Madam," I said, "I assure you, the boar will stop. Because it will never have seen anyone climb a tree so fast in all its life."

"Hmmph!" she said, and for a split second, something resembling a smile tried to cross her face, but was driven away before it could advance past the left cheek.

The silence rolled over me almost as soon as I left the yard. I had not realized how much Bors and his grandmother had pushed it back.

I climbed the hill behind the springhouse, sliding on the wet leaves. How had I never noticed how *quiet* it was before?

Granted, I probably wouldn't have noticed during that impossibly long January, and I had been a child for the majority of my visits before that. My sisters and I could certainly produce enough sound to drown out an approaching army. Had my parents sensed anything peculiar? Mother never said anything about it, although it was true that we hadn't come back after Father had died. Though presumably that was down to lack of money.

(Odd that she'd never sold the place. We could certainly have used the money. Even after I inherited my father's commission and swore as a soldier, my wage was only enough to keep the wolf from the door. It wasn't until my oldest sister wed that things settled down again.

Although selling property takes money and work, God knows, so it's very possible that she didn't have the money to pay the solicitors to wrangle the papers. I looked into buying a flat in Paris once and I think the papers cost more than the flat.)

I slunk between the tree trunks, trying not to skid on the mush of wet leaves, and looked for a gap in the trees, something that might lead to a clearing. I didn't have much hope of finding roe deer at this hour of the day, but still, one never knows one's luck. It did occur to me that possibly the deer would find the heavy quiet as oppressive as I did, but I dismissed it. The deer hadn't spent the last few years in Paris, and thus probably considered it a normal state of affairs.

I slipped and slid down the far side of the springhouse hill and halfway up the next one. The mist had mostly burned off, and I couldn't see the lodge behind me or the smoke rising from the chimney.

When a sound broke over me, shockingly loud, I nearly jumped out of my skin. I swung my rifle up instinctively, sighting down the barrel at the enemy, and . . .

"Caw," said the enemy agreeably.

I burst into slightly embarrassed laughter and lowered my gun. My heart thudded against my ribs.

The hooded crow—*kachulkni*, we call them here—looked down at me with the wary interest and mild pity that crows and ravens always seem to have for humanity. There were still a few leaves left on the trees, and I could just make out the bright eyes watching me between splashes of amber and gold.

I heard another *kachulkni*, cawing off in the distance, and listened to the breeze sighing through the leaves. Hearing it felt almost like when my tinnitus fades away and all the sounds come creeping back together.

Come to think of it, the silence was a *lot* like tinnitus. It rang in my ears the same way, drowning out everything around it, and making my thoughts echo unpleasantly inside my skull, as if every word was being read out just a little too slowly.

What if it wasn't the woods? What if it was me? Could this be some obnoxious new manifestation of my maladies—soldier's heart and battle nerves and whatever had gone wrong in my ears, between the cannon fire and the gunshots and that time back when I was young and foolish and kept a gun under my pillow and it went off an inch from my ear?

Christ's blood, that was an unpleasant thought. I kept telling myself that we'd be back in Paris as soon as the snow came, since Miss Potter could hardly hunt for mushrooms under such conditions, but what if going back to Paris didn't *fix* it? What if I leaned out my window and instead of hearing the lyrical sounds of cab drivers declaring blood feud on each other, there was only that smothering silence?

The crow launched itself into the air. I heard the snap of air against its feathers and then it cawed again and the sound felt like a benediction.

"Enough," I muttered to myself, deliberately speaking aloud. "You got used to your tinnitus, you'll get used to this. Assuming there's anything to get used to, and it's not just the woods or the altitude or a bit of bad sausage."

I set out deeper into the woods with a lighter heart. Tomorrow, in my experience, is only worth worrying about when there's something you can do about it. The sun was, for a wonder, shining, and even if it wasn't Paris, the woods of Gallacia were not a completely terrible place to be.

I had a lovely few hours hunting. I didn't actually bag anything, which is probably the reason that they were lovely. Once you've actually shot a deer, things tend to become very messy and practical and heavy and you have to start making calculations involving branches and leverage and innards. I was in a merry mood by the time I gave up and headed home and began singing that old Gallacian standard about the two drunk shepherds who sheared the bear. I am more enthusiastic than tuneful, but at least this way I wouldn't accidentally trip over a deer and ruin the hunting trip.

Practically between one word and the next, the silence rolled over me like a blanket of fog. The bright morning seemed to wash out around me, the sunlight leaching away. All the tiny bones in my ears, the ones that you never think about, suddenly felt individually swathed in wool. My singing faltered under the onslaught and fell flat.

Shit, I thought, and even thinking that took half a heartbeat longer than it should have.

Probably that was why I was just a hair too slow when my next step landed on a slick patch of leaves. I flailed my arms, skidded partway down the slope, almost caught myself, and then my other foot hooked a root and I went down like a felled tree.

5

"What happened to your trousers?" asked the Widow, as I slunk through the door in my mud-spattered finery.

"I fought a boar," I told her. "Single-handed. You were right, it laughed at the rifle, so I was forced to wrestle it in the mud."

"I know, Lord," said the Widow to the ceiling, "that You don't think much of liars. Thou shalt not bear false witness, You said, and—"

"I fell in the mud," I said, sighing. "I could save either my gun or my trousers, and my gun seemed more important."

This provoked a loud sniff, but she couldn't really argue with this decision. Trousers, after all, could be laundered. (Just try running a rifle through a mangle.) "I suppose you'll be wanting me to wash them for you."

"I would be most profoundly grateful, Mrs. Botezatu."

She took off her apron and picked up the buckets by the

door. "Just let me fetch some water from the stream, and I'll see if you've ruined them completely."

"The stream?" I blinked at her. "You don't use the springhouse?"

"I don't care for it," she snapped.

"But it's right by the back door—"

"I said, *I don't care for it.*" She picked up the buckets and stalked out of the kitchen.

I am, perhaps, not the sharpest bayonet on the battlefield, but even I know that if someone chooses to lug buckets of water a hundred yards rather than fifty feet, there's a stronger reason than a passing fancy. While I might be bit miffed that we'd done all that work scrubbing the springhouse out for nothing, what was I going to do, yell at her?

Anyway, never argue with your laundress. She has subtle and terrible ways of taking her revenge.

I had, fortunately, changed into clean trousers when I heard a "Halloo!" from the stableyard and came running down the steps, all thoughts of the springhouse and water preferences forgotten.

A coach was just leaving as I opened the door, and Angus was handing his horse off to Bors. Our visitor stood amid a modest pile of trunks and baggage.

Eugenia Potter looked just as she had when I saw her last: a sturdy, gray-haired Englishwoman, wearing very sensible waterproof boots. She inclined her head and gave me a small smile, which for the English upper classes was the equivalent of flinging her arms around my neck and pounding me on the back. "Lieutenant."

"Miss Potter." I bowed.

To my mild puzzlement, she pulled out a small book, peered at it, and nodded once. Then she said, in accented but quite clear Gallacian, "Easton, you young sinner! The Devil hasn't taken you yet, I see?"

My jaw sagged open. Bors, who was still in the stableyard, let out a single braying laugh and immediately slapped his hand over his mouth. Angus put his hand over his eyes.

"Oh dear," said Miss Potter, taking note of my expression. "Is my accent that bad?"

"No," I said, picking my chin up off my chest, "but who taught you to say that?"

She brandished the book at me. "This is the only Gallacian phrase book I have been able to locate. It described that as . . . let me see . . . 'a warm greeting suitable between two friends of equal social status.'"

"I have been telling Eugenia that the phrase book may not be entirely accurate," said Angus.

"Well, I suppose it wasn't *wrong*, exactly." I shook my head. "I . . . err . . . wouldn't use that one, Miss Potter. It's . . . ah . . ." I floundered for a phrase. "The sort of thing you'd say to a fellow drinker at a pub, say."

Miss Potter was clearly appalled by this, but rallied. "I *do* beg your pardon, Lieutenant."

"Not at all, not at all. I am delighted that we could provide you an opportunity to see the natural beauty of Gallacia."

"Especially the mushrooms," said Angus. I twitched.

"Oh yes!" Her face grew suddenly animated. "So many! I have been told that there are even *Boletus regius* to be found here, which are so dreadfully rare in Europe now."

"Are there?" I asked weakly, wondering what nightmarish fungus that might be.

"Certainly. A fir wood is just what it loves. I would dearly love to paint one." She rubbed her hands together. "And if there are any sheep meadows about, preferably very old ones, I am hopeful of finding earthtongues. The peak season will be coming on soon, and of course you can barely find them in England any longer."

"Earthtongues," I repeated. While I had not forgotten just how single-minded Miss Potter could be on the subject of mushrooms, I admit that time had softened my memory somewhat. "There are certainly sheep meadows about. Lots of them."

"Wonderful. If I can find a good specimen of the slimy earthtongue, I shall be most pleased."

"I'm sure that can be arranged," Angus said, with a light in his eyes that indicated he would scour the countryside until he had laid a slimy earthtongue at Miss Potter's feet.

Bors began carrying her trunks inside. I grabbed a suitcase and gestured to the door. "May I show you to your room?"

"Yes, thank you." She paused, gazing up at the lodge. "What a charming building!"

"Small, but it does for us," said Angus gruffly, but I could tell he was pleased.

"I hope you'll be comfortable here," I said.

"I'm certain I shall be. Truly, I should be grateful in far rougher surroundings, if it meant that I could spend time scouring your woodland for fungus. Why, in a forest like this, there could be as many as—"

I held up a hand. "Miss Potter," I said, with as much grace as I could muster, "you know that I am your devoted servant. I would travel to the farthest reaches of the globe if you asked. Your enemies are my enemies. I would fall upon my sword if I thought that I had contributed in the slightest to your unhappiness."

Miss Potter regarded me with knife-sharp eyes and said dryly, "I sense a 'but' coming, Lieutenant."

"Please, I beg of you. Do not tell me that there is fungus all around us. Do not remind me about spores in the water or myceli—myce—mushroom bits in the air. I cannot bear it. If you absolutely must tell me about an exciting mushroom, please start by telling me that it cannot possibly infect me or grow over me or poison me or . . . well, you know."

Her lips twitched. "The vast majority can do no such thing, I assure you."

I shook my head. It wasn't that I disbelieved her—Eugenia Potter was a true scientist, regardless of what the fossils at the Royal Mycology Society believed, and she learned more about fungus before breakfast than most of us would learn in a lifetime. Still.

"They truly don't bother you?" I asked. "Even after . . . ?" I didn't finish the sentence, but I knew that I didn't need to.

"Mycology is my life's work," said Miss Potter simply. "If a veterinarian dealt with a rabid wolf, no one would expect them to fear all animals afterward. So yes, even after . . ." She flapped a hand in the direction of the door, and presumably Ruravia and the dark tarn that had consumed the Usher house.

I sighed. Perhaps it was easier when you were a mycologist and saw the whole world in shades of fungi, and could easily differentiate between those that went into an omelet and those that consumed dead women's brains. Or possibly it was just the mycologist in question. "You are a braver soul than I am, Miss Potter."

She raised an eyebrow. "How many medals do you have in a box somewhere, Lieutenant?"

"Too many. They mostly don't hand those out for being brave, just for being too foolish to run away."

She pursed her lips and looked ready to argue, but I headed it off with a peace offering. "All that said, there's a mushroom in the springhouse. I don't know what it is, but I saved it for you when we cleaned it out."

"Come now," said Angus, "Miss Potter hasn't even unpacked. Don't go making work for her already."

"No, no." Miss Potter gave him a much warmer smile over her shoulder than I'd ever seen her give to anything that didn't have spores. "I'd rather look at it while the light is good. Unpacking is boring and easily done after dark."

We all tromped out to the springhouse. Even in the afternoon light, the interior was dark, but Miss Potter needed only a quick look. "Ah! A fine *Mycena* species."

"Amazing that you can tell all that at a glance," said Angus.

"Ah," said Miss Potter, "but this one, at least, is something any amateur could recognize." She reached down and plucked one of the small mushrooms up, carrying it into the light. "Observe, if you please."

We gathered around her, Angus besotted, me dubious, and Bors probably just wondering what we were blathering about. Miss Potter removed a pin from her hat and gouged the mushroom in its nasty pinkish cap.

It immediately began to bleed.

"Gah!" I said, taking a step back as the cap oozed a dark, syrupy red down onto her fingers.

"The common name is 'bleeding bonnets'," Miss Potter said. "This looks rather like *Mycena haematopus*, although those are more usually found on rotting wood. Hmm." She held it up, turning it this way and that. "A *sanguinolenta* would be more usual, given the location . . . though of course, that would not grow nearly so large . . ." She nodded to me. "An interesting specimen. I shall take a spore print."

Bors had been following this with interest, granted that he did not speak the language, and finally spoke up to say, "Is that not a blood-foot mushroom?"

"Is that what it's called here?" I asked weakly.

He nodded. "We do not eat them," he added. "They grow where the familiar sits."

Angus translated this for Miss Potter. "Like a witch's familiar, he means."

"There had better not be any familiars sitting around in my springhouse," I grumbled.

Angus snorted, but Bors gave me another grave nod. "If you bury a cat there, it will keep the spirits away."

"Nobody is burying a cat. I *like* cats."

"Not a living cat!" Bors was appalled that I would think he was perpetrating violence on innocent felines. "But perhaps there will be a cat in the village who has already died," he said. "You could purchase it."

I rubbed my forehead. "It's just a mushroom, Bors. We don't need to go buying deceased cats."

Bors actually looked disappointed, as if going to purchase a dead cat was a rare treat. Angus glanced over his shoulder at me and raised his eyebrows. I muttered something rude and followed him inside to dinner.

✳

Miss Potter and Widow Botezatu did not share a common language, but somehow they managed to communicate. Miss Potter's phrase-book Gallacian (vetted by Angus) was suitable for "please" and "thank you" and "May I help?" which were enough to endear her to the Widow. (I tried not to resent this. I said all those things too, but the Widow was never going to overlook my sin of being her employer. Miss Potter, being foreign, was shunted into the same category as children and innocents, and thus her virtues were greatly magnified and her failures easily overlooked. I was simply a bad Gallacian.)

It probably helped that Miss Potter did not demand English cooking and ate heartily of all the Widow's dishes, passing praise via Angus or myself. The quality of our food improved markedly. It hadn't been bad before, but it had been fairly monotonous. Now we only had paprika sausage for every *third* meal. (We stole that from the Hungarians, back when we tried to fight them and they beat us senseless. This is how Gallacia acquired most of its cuisine. The Widow made excellent paprika sausage, but one's bowels do require a few hours to recover now and again.)

Unfortunately, being suddenly held to higher standards did have its drawbacks.

"You'll be going to church tomorrow, of course," the Widow informed me, cornering me in my bedroom. I had been thinking of taking a nap, but she began cleaning aggressively around me.

"Errr . . . tomorrow?"

She skewered me with a look like a bayonet. "It's Sunday, innit?"

I had no idea if it was Sunday. Days at the lodge had all blurred together. "Oh, err, right. Sunday."

The Widow picked up my brush, untangled a few stray hairs from it, looked around for somewhere to dispose of them, then clucked her tongue. "Unlike some young wastrels I could name," she said to the ceiling, tucking them away in her apron,

"Miss Potter is a decent God-fearing woman and will doubtless wish to attend to her immortal soul."

"Oh, err, probably . . . ?"

Now, for the most part, I do not object to church. I think it's fine for those who want it. God, in my experience, is more likely to be found in gutters and at the bottom of dirty trenches than in designated architecture, but possibly that's just because that's where Ha is needed. (Ha and Har are our particular Gallacian pronouns that are used only for God. When I found out that in English those are sounds associated with laughter, all I could think was, "Yeah, sounds about right.")

Nevertheless, I do not believe that God cares where you worship Har. The prayers of the dying on the mud of the battlefield and the pleas of the fearful hiding in cellars must surely ascend just as quickly as those uttered under the light of stained glass. More quickly, if there is justice in the universe.

There was also the tiny matter that Miss Potter was probably Church of England and Gallacia is Catholic. Ish.

I opened my mouth to explain all this to the Widow, but what came out was, "I'll . . . err . . . go and ask?"

She folded her arms and glared, and I retreated with all speed.

✦

To my moderate dismay, Miss Potter announced that she would be delighted to attend services at a Gallacian church. "It'll be in Latin," I warned her.

"I know a fair amount of Latin, Lieutenant. I shall not take communion, for that would be theologically complicated, but I do not believe that God will object to me attending."

I heaved a sigh and resigned myself to getting up early for the liturgy.

Because Wolf's Ear was a good two miles away, we did indeed rise early. Bors had borrowed a donkey cart from somewhere and a donkey to go with it. He must have gotten up before dawn to fetch it. Both Miss Potter and the Widow rode with him, while Angus and I trailed like outriders watching for bandits. (We don't have that many bandits this far out of the capital. No one has enough to steal and everyone knows one another, so if you did ride up, pull a pistol, and shout, "Stand and deliver!" you'd most likely get a smack on the ear and dire warnings to tell your mother. Many a prospective bandit's career has been blighted by sheer embarrassment.)

There was a great deal of whispering and head-turning when we entered the church. Most of it was probably for Miss Potter, since being foreign is much more interesting than merely being an absentee landlord, but I still didn't enjoy it. I have never liked having large groups of people stare expectantly at me. It reminds me too much of my early days as an officer, back when I still thought that the rank and file expected officers to make sense. (I later learned that sergeants will handily translate anything you babble, but at the time, it was terrifying.)

I would have preferred to sit in the back of the church and bolt as soon as the service ended, but the Widow had other plans.

She had brought both a foreigner and the prodigal wastrel to church, and by God, she was going to make sure everyone saw. She herded us all to the second pew from the front and made certain that we genuflected properly on the way in.

The priest came out, greeted us all, and then launched into a great deal of Latin, then a sermon, which went in one ear and out the other. I believe it may have been about Maccabees. Then there was a great deal more Latin. My tinnitus kicked in about halfway through, but it didn't change anything much. I knelt when everyone else did, mumbled the responses, and tried to redeem myself by assisting the Widow in rising afterward.

We found ourselves in the line to speak to the priest after Mass. I saw that Miss Potter had her Gallacian phrase book in hand and winced in anticipation. "Remember that priests are addressed as *va* and *var*," I murmured in her ear.

She frowned down at the phrase book, then showed me a passage. "Is this an acceptable greeting?"

It translated roughly to *What trash has the wind blown in, then?* I shuddered and pointed to the next line down. Miss Potter mouthed it to herself, then nodded.

Fortunately she remembered the *va*, and even more fortunately, Father Sebastian turned out to be fluent in German, as was Miss Potter. Va listened to her halting greeting, replied politely, and then switched, which took the burden of translation off me and (more importantly) the phrase book.

Father Sebastian was tall, all squares and rectangles—

square beard, square shoulders, square and extremely thick eyebrows. "Forgive me," Miss Potter said to var. "I am attempting to learn Gallacian, but this phrase book I have found has proved . . . unreliable."

Va grinned at that. "We do not publish so many books in our native tongue," va said. "I have long wished to change that, but what with one thing and another . . ." Va spread var hands. "The Church sends me on rotation through four villages, a month at each one, and there is so little time for the writing of books. But it is a delight to practice my German again."

"But surely you must come and dine with us, Father," said Miss Potter, glancing at me to see if that was acceptable. I nodded affably. I have no objection to having a priest to dinner, so long as va does not attempt to turn the blessing into a lengthy sermon. "Then you may practice your German and I may try out my poor Gallacian on you."

"I would be most delighted," Father Sebastian said. Va considered briefly. "Would Tuesday be acceptable?"

"Allow me to ask the most important person involved," I said.

The Widow Botezatu, who had been observing this conversation between the priest and her pet foreigner with poorly hidden glee, was delighted at the prospect of feeding both at once, and readily agreed. We parted from Father Sebastian with a promise to see var in two days, and were finally allowed to leave the church and return to our usual week's degeneracy.

6

Tuesday rolled around and the Widow went into a flurry of cooking, as if expecting the priest to arrive with the entire royal family in tow. Father Sebastian brought only varself, which was good for dinner conversation but meant that we had food piled to the metaphorical rafters.

After dinner, we broke into the wine and, more importantly, the livrit. Miss Potter had never experienced livrit, and if we were good people, we would have allowed her to remain in that state of grace.

She sniffed her glass, held it at arm's length, and said, "In England, after dinner, traditionally the ladies retire to another room while the men drink. I have never approved of that tradition, but I am beginning to reconsider."

"You don't need to drink that," said Angus. "I am sure there is more wine—"

"Angus," she said, "I am a scientist, and what is science without bold experimentation?" And she tossed back about half the glass and set it down, with a light in her eyes and her lips firmly pressed together over a cough.

As difficult as it is to read Angus's emotions, I am fairly certain that he lost the remainder of his heart to Miss Potter in that instant. Father Sebastian and I let out a cheer. I offered to refill her glass, but she set her hand over it and shook her head.

"It was an *experience*," she said, only a little breathless. "I do not find myself needing to replicate that experiment, however."

Father Sebastian laughed. "You are an honorary Gallacian now," va told her.

"Good God, Father, why would you lay such a curse on her?" I made a sign to avert the evil eye, and heard the Widow snort audibly from the kitchen.

"I see that you have employed the Widow Botezatu," said Father Sebastian an hour or two later, once the Widow had informed us that we could clean up after ourselves because she was going to bed.

"Oh yes," I said, topping up var wine. "She has been taking excellent care of us."

"A most charming woman," va said, proving that even men of the cloth will lie when it suits them. "She has been a stalwart member of the parish for as long as I have served here."

"She is a fine cook as well," said Miss Potter. "I have not been so well fed in a long time."

I was at that pleasant stage of inebriation where I felt nothing but goodwill toward my fellow creatures. Still, it took me a moment to think of something nice to say about the Widow. I stared at the stuffed boar's head for inspiration.

"She's very brave."

All eyes turned toward me and I realized that I was going to have to explain. "Angus couldn't get anyone else to work here. All afraid of a . . . what was it? . . . moroi, if you can believe it. But not our Botezatu."

"Moroi?" asked Miss Potter. "What's that?"

"Monster that sits on your chest," I explained.

Miss Potter's head tilted to one side, like a very intelligent dog that has just watched you do something inexplicably foolish. "I beg your pardon?"

I shrugged helplessly, having exhausted my meager store of information about moroi. It was probably time I switched to water. "Sorry, I didn't hear the right stories growing up. Father Sebastian? Do you know?"

"I've heard of them, of course." Va gave me an apologetic glance. "I had even heard the rumors that there was one . . . errm . . . at large. Obviously I tried to dampen them, but there is only so much that one can do."

"Is this a local superstition?" asked Miss Potter.

"Not just local. You can find variations all across this part of Europe. The mare, the marra, the moroi . . . she has a very wide range." Va steepled var fingers. "A demon that comes in while you sleep and crouches atop your chest, stealing the breath from your lungs."

"Like an alb," said Miss Potter.

"Yes, much like that. Though the moroi, she is always female. She is often supposed to be like a werewolf, too, in that sometimes she is a living person who goes about at night."

Miss Potter shook her head sadly. "In my time in Ruravia— where I met my hosts, here—I heard stories of werewolves, but it did not seem as if they truly believed in them."

That was far from the worst thing she encountered in Ruravia, but I did not want to sour the wine in my stomach thinking about it. *I wonder if she's ever tried to tell anyone about the tarn? Would anyone believe it?*

"Gallacia is still steeped in the old ways," said Father Sebastian. "Very steeped. Do you know how Wolf's Ear got its name?"

Va addressed that last question toward me, and I had to admit that I didn't.

"Ah. The story goes that there was a town here with a different name, long ago, that was plagued by a werewolf. One night a man was walking home and was set upon by a wolf. He fought back and managed to cut its ear off. In the morning, the mayor was missing an ear. He tried to hide it, but the man nailed the wolf's ear to the door of the church, and by that, everyone knew that the mayor was a werewolf."

"Or he was simply very unlucky and lost an ear at exactly the wrong time," I muttered.

"Ah." The priest's lips twisted ruefully. "They thought of that. We are a practical people, are we not? They cut off his other ear first, and it, too, became the ear of a wolf, and so they drove him from the village with stones."

Miss Potter put a napkin to her lips. Father Sebastian was immediately contrite. "Forgive me, Miss Potter, for discussing such things in gentle company."

"No, not at all." She shook her head. "It was I who asked about werewolves. So does the moroi turn into a wolf as well?"

"Into a moth, if the stories are to be believed." Father Sebastian leaned back in var chair.

"Bit harder to cut the ear off a moth," observed Angus dispassionately.

"Indeed. And easier for the moth to slip into houses unobserved. I imagine most people would notice if a wolf was coming into their room at night. To stop a moroi, then, one must find who it actually is, if it is a living being." Va sighed. "I have been somewhat hard-pressed to stamp out that rumor. I do not want my parish turning on each other with such accusations. But they will not abandon their belief in the moroi, they will simply decide it is not a living being."

"I don't follow." I was starting to sober up, which was depressing.

Father Sebastian shrugged helplessly. "If she is not living, then she must be dead. Those are widely considered to be worse, because you can block up the entrance that a live moroi enters through, but if she is a ghost, she comes by way of your dreams, and how can you block the entrance to a dream?"

You can't, of course. There are dreams that I would wall off from myself if I could. I poured myself out a healthy measure of water. "Is that what they think happened to Codrin? A ghost came into his dreams?"

Father Sebastian sighed. "Toward the end, as he was dying, he started to hallucinate. You understand?"

"It takes people that way sometimes," said Angus gruffly.

The priest blinked, and I actually saw the moment that va remembered that Angus and I were soldiers. "Yes, of course. You would know." Va took a long swig of wine. "He was raving about the moroi sitting on his chest, taking his breath. And unfortunately there are those who sit up with the dying who . . . well, let us say the story spread, and not as the imaginings of a dying man."

I winced. I am no stranger to death, sad to say. Mostly the fast kind, at the end of a bullet or a mortar shell, but I've seen the slow kind often enough, as infection and wound fever takes its toll. Often enough, the dying saw things that weren't there. Sometimes it was the enemy, coming for them. Usually it was their mothers. Once or twice, something more dramatic. There was no rhyme or reason to it, not really. The most fanciful soldier I ever served beside was coldly lucid until kan heart stopped, and Sergeant Melisa, who had less imagination than a sheep, took two days to die and raved about angels and devils and spinning wheels of fire throughout.

To have someone spread tales of whatever Codrin ranted about in his final days seemed monstrously crass. What the dying say is between them and God.

"And now there's a rumor that this ghost is haunting people's dreams?" asked Miss Potter.

"So they say. She is supposed to come in the form of a moth or a beautiful woman. Though I think perhaps that last is mixed up with the tales of women who come at night to steal a man's . . . ah . . ." The priest suddenly remembered Miss Potter and coughed. Angus leaned forward and poured var more wine, while we all pretended that va hadn't been talking about wet dreams. (Not something I experience *personally*, you understand, but you don't live among soldiers who have their own slimy earthtongues popping up occasionally without getting a pretty good notion.)

"At *any* rate," va said, picking up the thread again, "the dead moroi are supposed to be the spirits of those buried in unconsecrated ground, without proper rites, trying to steal enough breath that they can live again. Sometimes it is even said that the moroi is the ghost of an unbaptized child or one stillborn, still trying to draw its first breath." Va sat up straighter. "*That*, of course, is pure nonsense. God is merciful and would never punish an infant so."

"But surely this is *all* nonsense," said Miss Potter. "You can't tell me that you believe in this . . . this base superstition!"

Father Sebastian raised var eyebrows, then smiled suddenly. "Do I believe that moroi are a real thing lurking about and sitting on people in the night? No, of course not. But as soon as the story went around the village, I had a dozen people telling me they dreamed of the moroi. The power of suggestion, as the mesmerists call it. But I cannot tell them that they are being silly, I can only tell them to trust in the Lord." Va gazed into var wineglass. "I have learned not to fight local superstitions. When I was barely out of seminary, I was assigned to a parish well south of here. They believed that the first day of the year that a shepherd led their flocks to pasture, they must go completely"—va glanced at Miss Potter and clearly changed what va was about to say—"*unclothed*. Otherwise sickness would follow the flock and kill many of them."

Miss Potter turned very slightly pink. Angus nodded to the priest and said, "Aye, they used to do that in my village as well."

"It does not surprise me. Well, obviously I tried to put a stop to it. It was indecent, and men and women both did it. Furthermore, it was generally still extremely cold, and they wouldn't even wear boots. One fellow was seventy years old, leading his sheep about, naked as the day he was born. It was only a matter of time before he caught his death."

"I'm guessing they didn't take kindly to that," said Angus, who was definitely smirking but managed to keep it all behind his mustache.

Father Sebastian nodded ruefully. "I thought I was making progress, but the bishop came down on my head and told me that I was on no account to interfere, or else the death of the sheep would be on my head. It turned out that he was *also* from a town where that was practiced. I have since learned to pick my battles." Va drained var wineglass.

Angus opened his mouth to say something, but stopped mid-word. A white moth had found one of the candles and was circling it, pale wings beating perilously close to the flame. All four of us watched it, torn between embarrassment and alarm.

"Shoo," I said, waving my hand at it. The candle flame bent in response. Wings kissed the back of my hand with a hint of moth dust, then it fluttered away into the darkness of the rafters.

"Well, this has all been fascinating, Father," said Miss Potter, breaking the uncomfortable silence. "I had no idea that local traditions were so . . . err . . . fraught." She smiled faintly. "In England, all we had were druids. And fairies, of course."

Angus didn't quite wince when she said *fairies* aloud, but he stilled just a little, as if hearing someone cock a gun in the distance.

"We've got those here too," I said. "Err . . . not the druids." I found myself reluctant to speak the word either. "In Gallacia, we call them the *other families*. They're supposed to lead people astray in the woods and . . . whatnot."

Miss Potter looked around the table as if she was waiting for one of us to start laughing. When no one did, she said, "Hmm."

"Speaking of going astray in the woods," said Father Sebastian, getting up, "I should be heading back before it gets too dark to see my hand in front of my face."

"You're welcome to stay here," I said.

Was there a shade of hesitation in var voice? "It's very kind of you to offer," the priest said, "but I really should be getting home."

*

That night, I dreamed of the moroi.

It began with two pale white threads snagged in a crack in my bedroom door. I lay in bed, watching them move restlessly, as if questing for something. Then a wriggle, a sideways motion, and a large moth pressed itself through the crack.

The moth fluttered through my bedroom, circling. It passed through the rack of antlers hung above the bed, alit for an instant on the sharp tip of one, then took flight again. It was silvery gray, shading to brown on its wings, the color of dried Gallacian clay. I saw a flash of flesh-colored stripes along its abdomen, and then it landed on my bed and became a woman.

She crouched on hands and knees beside me, looking down. Her skin was very pale and her eyelids had been painted dark colors.

She was neither beautiful nor ugly. In fact, she was plain and almost forgettable-looking—round face, snub nose, heavy eyelids. Some part of me found that extremely odd. If a moth is going to take the trouble to turn into a woman, you would expect her to look either hideous or inhumanly beautiful, not like any one of a hundred women that one might see on the streets of the capital.

I felt slow and stuporous with sleep, but I struggled to say something—anything—and finally came out with: "Pardon, mademoiselle, but I don't believe we've been introduced?"

She smiled slightly, or perhaps she had been smiling all along. Her lips were curved, though her eyes were sad. Basic chivalry compelled me to ask, "Is something wrong?"

She tilted her head, still with that small, sad smile, and leaned closer, almost within kissing distance. While I have occasionally kissed women that I haven't been introduced to, I do like to at least know their names if I'm in bed with them. (There was a slim possibility that I had known it, and had just forgotten, but it seemed unlikely. I don't actually go to bed with many strangers.)

I drew breath to ask her name again, and it didn't happen. Drawing breath, I mean. There was a weight pressing me down, and I realized that she was kneeling on my chest. I hadn't felt it happen, but now she was heavy, extremely heavy, and I could only get tiny sips of air.

I tried to reach for her, but my arms were pinned beneath the blanket. She watched me sadly. Clearly, she had no idea that she was crushing me. The dark room began to go darker, going silvery at the edge. *If I faint, we are both going to be so embarrassed.*

My tinnitus surged up then, ringing in my head like gunmetal bells. I winced, but it only rang louder, rising to that familiar tooth-aching whine—and suddenly I took a great gasping breath and sat bolt upright in bed.

It took a moment to catch my breath. The tinnitus slowly receded. I was in my bed, alone, with the sheets knotted around me, and a pounding headache that could easily be explained by the livrit.

7

The problem with telling a story, of course, is that you already *know* that I'm telling you about something significant that happened. It's not as if we sat down together and you said, "Alex, tell me a tale where you had a pleasant trip to your homeland and the worst menace you faced was the amount of paprika the Widow put in the sausages." No, you wanted a proper hair-raiser and here I am, trying to tell you one, whoever you are.

So of course, when you read me dreaming about the moroi, it seems significant. Doubtless I seem like a proper fool for not immediately packing up and going back to Paris. You can turn the page and assure yourself that you would be much wiser in my situation. (Quite possibly you would be. I've never claimed to be the sharpest tooth in the wolf's mouth.)

But for me, at the time, it was just a dream I had after heavy drinking and talking about a dream monster. The power of suggestion, as Father Sebastian had said. I got up and went downstairs and the Widow grumbled about young wastrels who slept until all hours, and I genuinely thought no more about it for quite some time.

We settled into a routine quickly enough. Miss Potter would go out early looking for mushrooms, with Angus accompanying her to fend off wolves, bears, and nefarious mushroom thieves. I would sleep until a decadent hour, get up, endure the Widow's comments on how it was all right for *some*, and engage in some general puttering around the lodge until Angus and Miss Potter returned for lunch, smiling and with flushed cheeks. (I assume this was from the late autumn chill. Certainly there was no other reason that they might be flushed. After all, we were carefully observing propriety.)

Bors would stop work for an hour when the sun was high, to avoid the attentions of the Noon Witch. (Do you have the Noon Witch in your country? She might be endemic to our region. She looks like a girl dressed in white, and she carries a scythe. If she talks to you while you are working, you must never try to change the subject or she will strike off your head or give you heatstroke. I've never heard of her appearing in the winter, as she's a demon of sunstroke, but obviously it was better to be safe than sorry.) Bors and I would play chess for an hour. I never won a game, but at least he had to work to beat me.

In the afternoons, Miss Potter would retire for a nap, and Angus and I would sit around in comfortable silence, reading whatever two-week-old paper he had managed to acquire in the village. I would take Hob out for a gallop if the weather allowed, and then we would have a pleasant meal, during which Miss Potter regaled us with their finds for the day, heavily annotated of course for my delicate antifungal sensibilities. She'd found her slimy earthtongue, which I was assured were harmless, if inedible, and I was treated to a discussion of the importance of the waxcap meadow environment. Into the evening, we would play cards, and Bors was willing to make a fourth for whist, provided that there was no actual gambling, and while he took a long time to make his plays, he was absolutely cutthroat once he did. It was like being bludgeoned to death by a cheerful turtle.

With a routine in place, my nerves began to settle. Even the occasional wall of silence was easy enough to shrug off. I went days without jumping at shadows, and my dreams were no more frightening than ever.

This pleasant state of affairs went on for about a week, until suddenly it didn't.

*

It was a wet, muddy morning that I came upon Bors splitting firewood in the yard.

He hadn't come in to play chess the last few days, and I had been wondering if I had offended him. He seemed to be moving slower than normal, and as I watched, he placed a section on the stump, lifted the axe, swung . . . and missed.

The blade struck badly off-center, skidded down, and buried itself in the dirt alongside his foot, nearly kissing the boot leather. A half-inch more and he would've been short several toes. "Bors!" I yelled, and he jerked back in surprise, lifting the axe, and very nearly put it in his own shin as the weight of the head dragged it down.

I grabbed the handle and took it away from him. "Bors, are you all right?"

He turned to face me, and I took an involuntary step back, still clutching the axe between us.

Bors was not all right. His eyes were huge and dark, and his face was drawn and waxy. The only color came from the circles under his eyes, which were bruised turquoise and violet with exhaustion. He looked more like a skull wearing makeup than a living man.

"Bors?"

"Sorry, Easton, sir," he mumbled, wiping at his forehead. "Haven't been sleeping well."

"You look *terrible*." I set the axe down.

"Sorry, sir."

"That's not a . . . I don't mean . . ." I flailed my hands. "You need rest! You're in no state to swing an axe around."

He peered vaguely around the stableyard. If it had been anyone else, I'd have thought he was nursing the hangover of a lifetime, but as far as I knew, the only alcohol that Bors had ever drunk was given to him by a priest, along with a very thin wafer and some Latin. "Not done working," he said.

"You're done for today. Go to bed." I tried to turn him toward the stable, but he resisted.

"Can't. Need to finish work." He swallowed. "Need to earn the wages."

"*Hang* the wages," I almost said, but bit it back. Easy for me to say, who was paying said wages, after all. Instead I said, "You've done the work of two men already this week. You've earned your wages clear through Sunday. Now go get some rest. That's your job for the rest of today."

His grandmother would have argued out of sheer pride, but Bors was either made of less stubborn stuff, or simply didn't have the energy to fight. He stumbled off toward the stable, and I followed far enough to make certain that he actually went into his room there, then went to tell the Widow. She muttered something about young men shirking work, but her heart clearly wasn't in it, given how quickly she shucked off her apron and went to check on him.

"How's Bors?" I asked the Widow the next morning as she transferred sausage from the frying pan to the plate.

"He's keeping." (Which, as I have already pointed out, could mean anything from a full recovery to being measured for a coffin.)

"Yes, but is he feeling better or . . . . ?"

"He's keeping well enough," she said, adding more words without any more information. She pushed the plate toward me. "Eat. I'll not be making you up another breakfast if you let this one get cold."

I took my plate, bolted my breakfast, and decided to go check on the patient myself.

The door to his room was ajar. Oddly enough, someone had shoved a handkerchief into the keyhole. I was staring at it, hanging there like a little white flag of surrender, when I heard a gasping moan from inside.

"Bors? Are you all right?" I peered around the doorframe and saw him, a humped shape under the blankets. His breathing was labored and painful, as if a corner of the blanket had gotten into his mouth. I didn't want to go and shake him, though—that seemed a rather aggressive intimacy. I tried raising my voice. "*Bors?*"

He sat up and sucked in his breath in a harsh gasp, then broke into a coughing fit. I stepped into the room and began pounding him on the back. "Steady on, old fellow. Something go down the wrong pipe?"

"Sorry, sir," he mumbled. "Is it time for work?" He shook his head and coughed again. "I'm sorry, I'm just so tired . . ."

"No work for you today," I said, with false heartiness. He looked dreadful. I've seen dead men with better color. "You just focus on getting better. I'll send your grandmother in with some tea and breakfast, shall I?"

"Yes, sir." He sank back to the mattress, looking around the room in bleary confusion. I still wasn't certain if waking him up was the right thing to do or not, but I hadn't liked the way his breathing sounded. It put me in mind of my own dream the other night, when I had awoken, unable to catch my breath—but no, that had gone away in a moment or two, nothing like this. I shook off the thought and told myself sternly that Bors was the one who was ill and that I was much too old to be making things all about myself.

At least Bors was breathing easier now. I went inside to fetch the Widow.

And you may call me a fool if you like, because even then, I didn't think of Codrin.

8

Bors was no better the next day. I found him asleep, sitting upright next to the springhouse, with a bucket in his lap. When I woke him, he jumped, shocked, and looked at me from dark-circled eyes. "Oh! Sir! I'm sorry—I just sat down for a moment—"

"Bors," I said sternly, taking the bucket, "you should be very sorry. I definitely did not give you permission to go back to work. It's freezing out here. Come on, lean on me, let's get you back down the hill."

He protested weakly, but he was in no shape to stop me from taking the bucket. He wasn't feverish at least, that much I could tell from supporting him on the way back. Since sleeping seemed to be anathema—or perhaps he was simply bored to tears—I saw him tucked up in the lodge, near the fire, with a couple of bridles. "Here," I said. "Check these over and mend any worn spots."

"I'll get oil on the blanket," he mumbled.

"Then I shall fetch you a saddle blanket." Which I did. Then I made tea, because even if I couldn't have hot tea on hand every minute of the day, like Codrin had, I could still boil up something.

Codrin had been alone in the house when his lungs had begun to fail him. What must that have been like? He and Bors were cut from the same uncomplaining cloth. I could all too easily imagine him trying to work, as Bors was, without anyone on hand to tell him to sit down and *rest*, goddammit.

My thoughts circled Codrin as I waited for the kettle to heat up. Had he been frightened? Had he suspected that he was dying?

Could Bors be . . . ?

Not on my watch, I thought grimly.

I found the Widow in the pantry, measuring out a cup of salt, and said, with my usual delicacy and tact, "I think we should fetch a doctor for Bors."

"A doctor!" The Widow looked at me as if I'd suggested sending for the hangman. "D'you want him to *die*?"

"That is the exact opposite of what I want . . . ?"

She sniffed and pushed past me, still carrying the salt. "The doctor! Might as well put him in the ground and save the money."

That bit I understood. I rubbed the back of my neck. "Mrs. Botezatu, I'd be more than happy to pay for it—"

"Can You believe this, Lord?" she asked the ceiling. "Young wastrels offering to pay doctors. As well hire an assassin, as well You know."

"Mrs. Botezatu—"

She picked up a carving knife. Fortunately the kettle went off at that moment and she took over making tea before I could find out just what she planned to use that knife for, or what strange recipe required an entire heaping cup of salt.

*

It was a long day, made longer by worrying. I have seen too many people take ill, and too many of those didn't recover. I told myself that most of those people had been shot and picked up an infection afterward, which is totally different than whatever was troubling Bors. Then I told myself that this was absolutely nothing like what happened to my old friend Madeline Usher, there was not even a trace of catalepsy involved, and it was ridiculous to even think of such things.

Then I drank too much, although I retained enough decency to wait until after dinner so as not to embarrass myself in front of Miss Potter.

When I finally made my way to bed, I sank into the mattress, shoved my arm under the pillow—and promptly let out a bellow as something stabbed me.

Angus was in the doorway, his pistol at the ready, by the time I got the lamp lit. My knuckles were leaking blood and my nightshirt was splattered with red, but there was no one else in the room.

"Why, in the name of Saint Elias's blighted left nut," I snarled, "was there a *knife* under my *pillow*?!"

There is nothing quite like being stabbed to sober one up

quickly. Angus looked at the knife. It was the sort you'd use to cut fruit. It had carved quite a nice divot out from between my first and second knuckles.

Miss Potter appeared behind Angus. "Easton?" she asked groggily. "What's going on?"

My duty as a host rose up and strangled my outrage. "Forgive me, Miss Potter," I said, bleeding with as much dignity as I could muster. "I did not mean to wake you." I closed my eyes briefly, struck by a sudden dreadful suspicion. "Is there . . . by chance . . . any cutlery under your pillow?"

". . . Cutlery," said Miss Potter.

"I'm afraid so."

In Miss Potter, the legendary stiff upper lip of the British was cast in steel. She nodded as if this was a perfectly normal request, returned to her room, and reappeared a moment later, holding a very large butcher knife. Her expression wavered between "this is arguably somewhat peculiar" and "of course, all the best people keep knives in the bed." At the moment, *peculiar* was winning, but only just.

Angus muttered something under his mustache and went to his own room. He came out holding a bread knife. "Under the pillow," he confirmed.

There was only one possible culprit, of course.

"The *Widow* did this," I said. The knife lay beside my pillow, with a bit of my flesh clinging to it like the skin of a melon.

"But *why* are there knives under the pillows?" asked Miss Potter.

"That is an excellent question," I said through my teeth.

"It's an old superstition," said Angus. "Iron under your pillow wards off evil."

"Ah," said Miss Potter.

"But what was she—" I clamped my mouth shut on the next words. I did not want to know what evil the Widow feared. What I *wanted* was to go downstairs, roust the Widow, and give her the sort of dressing-down that the enlisted would speak of in hushed voices for years to come.

Which would accomplish . . . exactly nothing. I could hardly threaten to bust her back down to private, and I would have felt monstrous firing the Widow Botezatu. She obviously needed the wage, as did Bors. They were poor as church mice, but the Widow would take charity when hell froze over and the dead sang hosannas at the Second Coming.

"Right," I said. "I suppose we'll just . . . go to back to bed then, shall we? I apologize for having woken you all."

"I appreciate the warning," said Miss Potter graciously, gazing at her knife. I noticed absently that the Widow had given her the biggest knife in the kitchen. Obviously Miss Potter warranted the very best.

"Let's wrap up that hand first," said Angus.

I submitted to this with less than perfect grace, but of course it's very hard to bandage your own hand. I washed it in the basin, which hurt more than the initial stabbing, then Angus wrapped it in a couple of layers of bandage. I stared upward, which is how

I noticed that the rack of antlers now bore a cat's cradle of red thread. I realized that I could not possibly deal with that in my current state and transferred my gaze to the wall.

"She meant well," said Angus, when he had tucked the ends under. "She's worried."

"About what?" I snapped. "Moroi or werewolves or whatever it was?"

"Naturally."

His matter-of-fact answer brought me up short. My eyes drifted to the red thread above me. "But that's nonsense. You *know* it's just superstition."

"Witch-hares are just superstition too."

I recoiled as if I'd been slapped. In Ruravia, there were legends of witch-hares. What we'd found when we opened up a dead one had been far worse.

"I'm not saying what it is or isn't," said Angus, getting to his feet. "I'm saying that the Widow isn't a fool, and she's worried. Which makes *me* worried."

He didn't add *And you ought to be worried too.* He didn't have to.

I stared up at the ceiling in the dark, listening to the silence and wondering if I was a fool.

✳

I woke much too early in the morning and discovered that it was beginning to snow. If I'd thought for a minute that this meant the end of our sojourn in Gallacia, I might have rejoiced, but alas, it was the kind of snow that you get around here in autumn, where it falls as flakes, hits warm ground, and melts immediately. We could still have several weeks left before the ground actually froze, which meant that there would be plenty of time yet for mushrooms.

Anyway, if I turned tail and ran for Paris, Bors would still be here without a doctor.

Probably he'd recover just fine, of course.

Likely it was only a cold.

There was no reason to feel responsible, except that I had money for a doctor and the Widow didn't, and goddammit, what if I could *fix* this? There are so few things in the world that I can fix.

One of those things may or may not be knives under pillows in the night.

Moroi. I had spent half the night arguing with myself about whether or not such things could exist. In the gritty light of dawn, it all seemed ridiculous. Women who turned into moths to haunt your dreams? No wonder Meriam had slammed the door on me, if she'd been hearing people spout such nonsense since her father's death.

I entered the kitchen and found the Widow engaged in the alchemy that turns large bones into delicious stock. I understand how it all works, but it did look rather as if she were throwing the remains of some unfortunate soul into a stewpot. Nevertheless . . .

"Mrs. Botezatu," I said, with wonderful calm, "did you know that there were knives under our pillows last night?"

"Put them there yesterday," she said, as if this should be blindingly obvious.

"I am afraid I stabbed myself."

She stopped, turned, and stuck out her hand. I stared at the hand, not sure what I was supposed to do, and she snapped her fingers and wriggled them impatiently. I eventually realized that I was supposed to show her my injury.

"Hmmph!" she said, when she could not find immediate fault with Angus's doctoring.

"Now, surely you must see that there's no reason to put . . ."

"I'll mix up some honey and an onion," she said, ignoring my attempts at firmness. (Honey and onion is an old Gallacian cure-all for all external injuries. For internal injuries, remove the onion and add livrit instead.)

"Really, there's no need . . ."

"And I'll need those knives back for the cooking, mind. You can have them tonight."

"Ah, I'm not sure if . . ."

An hour later, Angus found me lurking in the stable. Hob had gotten some tangles in his mane and I was brushing them out, trying not to make any noise that might disturb Bors. He was still dead to the world, and I was inclined to let the poor man sleep.

"What happened to you?" he whispered. "And what is that *smell*?"

"The Widow happened."

"Ah." He craned his neck past me. "Bors still asleep?"

"I certainly hope so." I fancied I could hear the rattle of his breath from here. "I wish the Widow would let me send for a doctor, but whenever I suggest it, she acts like I want to take Bors out behind the barn and shoot him."

"Ah, well, you know how some people are. They don't send for the doctor until it's far too late for one to help, so of course doctors must be useless and just hasten the dying. My own family was the same way."

"Angus," I said.

"Hmm?"

"*You're* the same way. I practically had to sit on you that time you broke your ribs. You kept saying you'd walk it off."

"And what good did the doctor do me? I was already wrapping it and had a good goose-grease plaster to draw out the pain."

"He gave you pills for the pain. And the apartment smelled like mustard and dead goose for a *month*."

Angus's mustache appeared unconvinced, but he changed the subject. "At *any* rate, we were talking about the Widow, not me. Have you considered sending for the priest? Might be that va could convince her."

This struck me as a marvelously sensible plan. In fact, if I was lucky, va might put the Widow's mind at ease about moroi. And Angus's mind. Possibly my mind as well. I combed the last tangle loose from Hob's mane and picked the stray hairs loose from the brush. That reminded me of something, but I couldn't place it. I stared at the long, silky hairs, then at my bandaged hand, and

thought of knives and honey and onions. "Father Sebastian is a
brilliant idea. I don't know how much more of this I can take."

Angus began saddling the horses. I slipped into the room
at the end of the stable and found Bors propped up on pillows,
looking like lukewarm death.

"Bors?"

"Mmm?" He looked at me blearily.

"How are you feeling? And don't say, 'I'm keeping.'"

He managed a wan smile. "Like there's . . . something heavy—"
He sucked in a shallow, rattling breath. "—on my chest."

The hag that sits on your chest. I scowled at the thought, and
Bors gave me a worried look. "Is there . . . something that . . .
needs doing?" He struggled to sit up farther.

"No! Not at all. We were thinking of going into town. Do
you need anything?"

He shook his head. I wondered if there was a knife under
his pillow. Given how the Widow had been acting, I wouldn't
be surprised if there was an entire armory.

"Right," I said. "I'm going to try to get a doctor for you.
Don't tell your grandmother."

Bors nodded. I turned to go, but his next words stopped me.
"Grandmother says . . . I have to fight her . . . but I'm no good
at fighting . . . never was . . ."

"Fight her? Fight who?"

He closed his eyes, losing the battle with sleep. "That
woman . . . in my dreams . . ."

9

Miss Potter insisted on going into town with us, but as we did not have the wagon—obviously no one was going to ask Bors to go borrow it, and I certainly wasn't going to turn up at a stranger's farm and ask them to loan me a wagon and donkey—she rode double with Angus. As a result, I deliberately rode well behind them, letting Hob follow Angus's horse but not intruding too close on the pair. At least *someone* was enjoying themselves.

The snow continued to fall. It hissed a little as it hit the leaves, but still wasn't building up. It was certainly much more pleasant to ride through than rain would be. I let my chin drop to my chest while the world went pale and blurry and softly muffled around me.

At some point during the ride, I slipped back into the war.

It wasn't bad. I don't want you to think that every time I

visit the war, I'm instantly thrown into a battle. Honestly, it's usually not like that. I was just riding along, half dozing, secure in the knowledge that this was all friendly territory and the front was many miles away. Skipper was under me and he was an old campaigner and would let me know if there was anything I needed to be worried about. (That's one of the rules you learn as a cavalry scout, if you don't want to burn out hard and fast: Trust your horse to tell you when to pay attention.)

If you'd asked me, I could have told you that I was in Gallacia. I could remember that I'd lost Skipper years ago when he put his foot in a rabbit hole, and that there wasn't a front. But those were merely facts and they didn't change what I *knew*, half awake as I was.

Because of what I knew, when I heard a voice ahead, my first thought was "Why is Miss Potter here in Serbia?" I looked down and my horse was bay instead of gray, and of course he was Hob, not Skipper, and then I shook myself and sat up a little straighter, and the war receded behind me.

I sometimes think the fundamental disconnect with civilians is that they think a war is an *event*, something neatly bounded on either end by dates. What anyone who's lived through one can tell you is that it's actually a place. You're there and then you leave, but places don't stop existing just because you aren't looking at them.

The war's still there. I don't live in it anymore, but it's right over there, just on the other side of . . . I don't know. Something.

Maybe the mystic veil that the spiritualists are always going on about, except there's nothing mystic about it.

And sometimes, for a little while, I slip over into that other place. The war.

It's not like just remembering something bad. I have plenty of bad memories, many of them related to the war, in fact, but remembering them doesn't mean I'm *there*, any more than remembering that I had the flu as a child means that I run a fever now. This is more like rounding a corner and finding myself unexpectedly in a familiar neighborhood. It's a place I go to, even if nobody else can see that I've gone. I can smell it and certainly hear it, even if I can't always see it.

That's the problem with all those well-meaning people who try to comfort you by telling you that everything's okay, you're home now, and the war's *over*, as if you're an idiot who can't read a newspaper and see that an armistice has been declared. It's like telling someone that Greece is over, or England, or Russia. It's nonsensical. Places aren't ever *over*, except maybe Pompeii.

Still, we pretend to believe it, all of us who sometimes fall over into that familiar place. Trying to explain that the war will never *be* over just makes you sound either mad or self-pitying, and makes your relatives look at you worriedly and pat your hand, and that's far more exhausting. You learn to just smooth over the conversation and get on with things. It doesn't even feel like a lie.

As long as you don't hurt anybody and don't act too obviously strange, most people will let it go. The other ones like you understand. We all realized long ago that we're dual citizens now, that we come from two different places.

Gallacia. And the war.

*

Father Sebastian was staying in a tiny one-room building near the church. You couldn't really call it a rectory. When the three of us knocked on the door and va invited us in out of the snow, we filled it to overflowing. The walls were whitewashed and a crucifix hung on the wall. It reminded me of Codrin's room, the same sense of someone living there but barely leaving a mark. Father Sebastian traveled between parishes, so va had an excuse. I still wasn't sure about Codrin.

"Miss Potter, Lieutenant Easton . . . Mr. Angus . . ." (No one knows Angus's last name. I don't even know it, and I've known him my entire life.) "A pleasure to see you all again. Err . . . are you seeking spiritual counsel?"

"Something like that," I said, and launched into the saga of the Widow Botezatu, the knives under the pillows, and, of course, Bors's illness.

The priest listened gravely to this, although va did have a suspicious coughing fit when I recounted gouging myself on the knife. "Sharp steel under the pillow," va said. "A common superstition hereabouts."

I raked my hands through my hair. "Does *no one* here put their arms under their pillows at night?!"

"I imagine that you quickly learn not to," Father Sebastian said mildly, although I could tell va was trying not to laugh. "Given the stabbing and all." Va drummed var fingers on the small table. "I am afraid that even if I suggest very strongly that the Widow sends for the doctor, it won't do much good. People seem to either believe that a doctor should come at all hours to attend their slightest sniffle, or that they are omens of death, with no ground in between."

"But surely there must be something we can do?" said Miss Potter. "The poor young man looks half dead."

Father Sebastian got up, possibly intending to pace back and forth, only to discover that there was no room to do so with three extra people in the room. Va ended up making a rather tight circle, then sinking back into the chair. "Perhaps . . . hmm. I have one idea. The doctor speaks German, as it happens. Would you care to invite us both to dinner, to work on our vocabulary? If nothing else, once he is in the house, he can look this young fellow over, and perhaps he'll be able to suggest something else."

"Admirably sneaky for a man of the cloth," I said. "Please, Father Sebastian, would you come to dinner at the lodge? As soon as you can, and bring this doctor friend with you."

"I would be honored," Father Sebastian said, bowing slightly. "Shall we say tomorrow night?"

As we were leaving, I paused on the threshold. "Father? Do you know if red thread is supposed to keep anything away?"

Va frowned at me. "Red thread? I know some people hang that around baby's cradles to keep them from being stolen by the . . . ah . . . other families."

"Ah. Thank you."

The priest nodded. "Rank superstition, of course," va said, after a moment, but I don't think var heart was in it.

✳

Our part in the plan was easy enough. I told the Widow that the priest was coming to dinner and bringing a friend, and she told the ceiling that it was apparently her lot in life to prepare feasts on a moment's notice, but as this was God's chosen representative, she would not begrudge it.

Unexpectedly, the ceiling answered, although in the voice of Miss Potter. "Bors? What's wrong?"

The Widow and I scrambled up the stairs to find Miss Potter in the upstairs hall. She stepped aside to reveal Bors standing, facing the wall. His eyes were closed, but as we watched, he reached out one hand and hesitantly pushed against it, almost as if he expected it to open like a door.

His fingertips had turned a sickly reddish-violet shade that stood out starkly against the whitewash. "My God, man!" I said involuntarily.

The Widow's glare could have stripped paint, and too late I remembered the belief that if you wake a sleepwalker, their soul might never come back. "Sorry," I mumbled, stepping back. She signed the cross hastily in the air, encompassing herself, Bors, and Miss Potter.

Bors opened bloodshot eyes. "Where did . . . ?" he asked blearily.

"Hush," said the Widow, slipping under his arm. "You're dreaming, child, that's all. Let's get you back downstairs."

Miss Potter gave me a worried look over the man's head. Whatever was happening, Bors seemed to be going downhill rapidly.

"Let's take him to my room instead," I said. "He doesn't need to be sleeping in a drafty stable in this condition." I took his other side, supporting most of his weight. The Widow was as tough as old roots, but her grandson was at least twice her size. "Miss Potter, will you find Angus?"

"But sir . . ." Bors struggled feebly as he realized where we were taking him. "I can't take your bed."

"Absolutely you can. I'll bed down in the stable." He tried to protest again as Angus appeared and wrestled his shoes off, but I held up a hand. "Hush, Bors, it's a far better bed than I ever had out on campaign."

"But . . . ."

I might have lost the argument, but the Widow backed me up. The color of Bors's lips probably had something to do with it. Against his grandmother, Bors had no chance, and we pulled the covers up over him and the Widow went off to make something foul-smelling on the stove. I was pressed into service to go and acquire goose grease from the village, which I did, mostly by wandering through the market looking helpless until someone took pity on me.

That evening, when I went out to the tack room in the stable where Bors had been sleeping, I discovered a thick white line across the threshold. I stared at it for a moment, then stirred it with the toe of my boot. It crunched slightly. Snow? No, snow didn't fall in lines, indoors. I crouched down and picked up a pinch of fine white crystals, then touched one to my tongue.

Salt.

All at once I remembered the Widow with her heaping cup of salt. Another one of her wards against evil, no doubt. I lifted my head and saw that the handkerchief was still in the keyhole. I yanked it out, annoyed. *Salt on the floor, threads on the walls, and iron under the pillow, but God forbid we call a doctor to actually listen to her grandson's lungs . . .*

The room wasn't bad. Most of the stable wasn't heated, of course, but this room had a tiny stove in it. It wasn't quite cold enough for me to bother with that, so I carried a hot brick in from the fire for my feet, piled a great many blankets on myself, and went to sleep.

Somewhere in the night, I woke myself up, unable to fully breathe. I choked for a moment, pawing for my face, and realized that I had pulled a blanket over my head. I dragged it down, letting the cold air hit my skin, and took a deep breath. "Heh," I said out loud.

At least, I *thought* I said it out loud.

I couldn't hear myself speak. I heard the words inside my head, felt their resonance in the bones of my skull, but nothing passed my lips.

I blinked against the darkness and the silence covered me, more thickly than the blankets, muffling everything.

Slowly the ceiling came into focus, a bare sketch of rafters against the shadows. I turned my head (the sheets should have rustled, but did not) and saw the little sliver of moonlight through the closed shutters, which left a thin blue bar across the blankets. I followed the bar of light to the woman who sat on the side of my bed, watching me.

My whole body jerked with surprise. *Damnation.* If she was an enemy, I should not have given any sign that I was awake and aware. But that was no longer an option, so I tried to brazen it out. "Excuse me, madame—" I began, and the silence plucked the words away.

The woman looked at me with a small, sad smile. She had a round face and a snub nose, and looked familiar somehow. Did I know her from somewhere? It seemed like I should recognize her. I tried again. "Have we been introduced?"

It was as pointless to speak the second time. She held a finger to her lips, which also seemed pointless. No one could hear me, wasn't it obvious?

Unless she *could* hear me, and it was only my ears that were failing?

"Can you hear me?"

She didn't make any sign that she could. She was sitting close enough now that I could see individual strands of hair falling over her face. Had she moved closer? I didn't remember that. Her smile was the same. I suppose I'd say it was wistful, except that I never think of things being wistful, and at the moment I was much more concerned with the fact that I couldn't hear anything.

There is a particular way that I can flex the muscles of my jaw that will often set off a bout of tinnitus. (Conversely, I sometimes realize that what's setting off a bout is the fact that I'm clenching my jaw.) I tried it now. Surely if the silence was somehow the next stage of the tinnitus, I couldn't just go back to the first one, right?

It made sense in my head, barely, but it didn't work, at least at first. I ground my teeth until I thought they'd splinter. The woman leaned over me, one hand on my chest, pressing down. Her eyelids were as black as bruises. Her hand was very heavy and who was this strange woman touching me anyway, although maybe she wasn't strange, maybe she *was* familiar and I had drunk too much again . . .

A roar started in my ears, climbing to a high mosquito whine. It was all in my head, but it drove out the awful unfamiliar silence and replaced it with awful familiar noise. I nearly sobbed with relief, and at first I couldn't hear that either, but then the whine began to fade and I caught the tail end of my own breathing and when I opened my eyes, there was no woman, and the blue bar of moonlight lay untroubled across my bed.

I lay against the pillow, gasping. My chest ached as if I'd been running. Christ's blood, was I catching whatever Bors had?

No, it was a dream. You're breathing fine now, see? Just a dream. Like that other dream, with the moth who turned into a woman. She seemed familiar too, didn't she?

Was it the same woman? I tried to call up the image, but it was already unraveling, as dreams do, and I could not quite picture her face.

I lay in bed for a few minutes longer, then got up. I groped around until I found the handkerchief and, deeply annoyed with myself, shoved it back into the keyhole.

10

Bors actually did look better in the morning. His lips no longer had that blue tint and although he yawned a great deal, he didn't seem in danger of falling asleep instantly. He said something about giving me my bed back and I shot that suggestion down immediately. "Not while the room smells of goose grease and camphor," I said. "You're stuck here until the smell's gone."

The Widow was, of course, aware of all this, and took her gratitude out on me in the form of rubbery eggs and burnt toast, which I ate anyway. After breakfast, I got on a chair and took down the red thread that had somehow made its way across the antlers on the wall. The Widow would probably rehang it within a day, but I drew the line at having dinner guests in a room that looked as if it was draped in bloody cobwebs.

"There are no children here for anyone to steal away," I muttered, unwinding thread from around the tusks of the boar.

"Is she just doing everything she knows and hoping something works?" (That actually did make sense. I wondered how many things I hadn't noticed. Come to think of it, she'd scattered rue in the corners a few days earlier, and told me it kept away mice. Though then again, it might, what do I know?)

Father Sebastian arrived a little after teatime, with a tall, dark-haired man in tow. Dr. Virtanen was Finnish, as it turned out, and spoke Gallacian very well, probably because his language was almost as miserably complicated as ours. His German was also substantially better than mine, particularly in scientific terms, and he and Miss Potter were soon chatting away about mushrooms and mycology and various other things that I could only partly understand.

The Widow froze when she saw him, then turned a hostile glare on me. I did my best "too dim to notice" expression, which Angus tells me I am particularly adept at, but she grabbed the air above my shirtsleeve, which froze me immediately in place. (The next step would have been to actually lay hold of me, and I don't know if either of us could have borne the escalation.) "I told you not to send for him!" she hissed.

"He's not here for Bors," I lied. "He's here to speak German with Miss Potter."

She inhaled sharply through her nose. I could tell that she didn't quite believe me, so I added, "Father Sebastian brought him. They're friends."

The Widow could not bring herself to slander a priest in front of me, although I was certain she'd have a few choice words for God later. She nodded stiffly and stepped back, returning to the kitchen and slamming skillets around with more than her usual vigor. This environment was not terribly conducive to conversation, so we went outside and stood around in the courtyard. *Courtyard* is probably an overly grandiose term for the triangle formed between the house and the stable and the hill with the springhouse, particularly when it was muddy from rain and full of wood chips from the firewood stump. When I hear *courtyard*, I think of hedges and topiary. I was certainly not a topiary sort of person, and the previous owners of the lodge hadn't been either.

Nevertheless, it was pleasant enough, particularly with drinks to ward off the chill in the air. We watched the sun set behind the trees, painting a brief, bloody light along the springhouse roof, and talked about the difficulties of property upkeep, while the shadows diffused into dusk and white moths battered themselves against the windows of the lodge.

Dr. Virtanen was a fine guest, possessing good conversation and a quiet wit. He'd fallen in love with a Gallacian girl and moved down here years ago, setting up his shingle and raising a family in one of the nearby towns. I liked him, but then again, I've always had a soft spot for Finns. Some claim they're unfriendly, but every one that I've ever met has been quite pleasant, if reserved. They have the quiet confidence of a people who know that, at any moment, they could strap on skis, go into the woods, and take out an entire squad of enemy soldiers before anyone knows they're there.

Also they're the only country I know whose national liquor is worse than ours. I know, because Dr. Virtanen brought a bottle of salmiakki liqueur with him as a gift. He said it would keep out the chill, and it did. No chill could possibly fight its way through that much black licorice.

Dinner that night was particularly lavish, the Widow apparently feeling that the doctor was a worthy enemy and thus should be fed until he damn well choked. I made a note to bring enemies to dinner more often.

After dinner, Father Sebastian asked after Bors and the Widow led var to the bedroom. "Not feeling well, eh?" the priest said. "Dr. Virtanen, you know these things. Is something going around?"

"Ah, well," the doctor said from the doorway. "I haven't brought my full kit, I'm afraid, but of course it's fall, and you know how the damp air gets into the lungs. Coughing, are you, young man?"

"Not much. Hard to breathe, though," Bors admitted. "At night, especially."

"Sauna, that's what you need," Virtanen said, thumping himself on the chest. "Clear everything out. Sauna and vodka will cure more things than doctors." He winked at the Widow, who was hovering nearby. "Failing that, listen to your grandmother here. I'll wager she knows her way around a mustard plaster, eh?"

The Widow unbent enough to admit that she might possibly be familiar with such a thing.

"There, you see?"

Bors said something else, too quietly for me to catch, but

Virtanen said, "No surprise there. The body affects the mind, so you'll have strange dreams when you're sick. If you're not up and around in a few days, send for me, and perhaps I can think of some trifling thing that might help, but the best cure is usually fresh air and rest."

He came downstairs and we all pretended we hadn't been eavesdropping in the hallway. Father Sebastian stayed with Bors to take his confession or offer him spiritual counsel or whatever priests do when they visit the sick.

"I wouldn't worry about tuberculosis unless it goes on for another few weeks," Dr. Virtanen murmured in an undertone. "But if he starts coughing more, or coughing up blood, call for me at once. Odds are good it's nothing more than a passing infection of the lungs, but there's always a chance . . ." He spread his hands.

"I doubt Mrs. Botezatu will let us send for you," I said glumly. "She thinks doctors are a type of undertaker."

He smiled ruefully. "A common enough belief locally. Worse if one is a foreigner. Though you might consider building a sauna. It won't hurt, and even if it doesn't help, at least then you'll have a sauna."

Which, as medical advice goes, was not the worst I'd ever heard by a long shot.

Bors was no better the next morning, and the Widow was quietly furious that I'd brought a doctor in and made a priest party to my deception.

"He didn't actually do anything," I protested, as she growled at God about my transgressions. "And he said it didn't sound like tuberculosis."

If she hadn't been indoors, I think she would have spat. "Tuberculosis! Even a useless carrion crow of a doctor could tell that."

I gave up. I had no idea what would make her happy, or what I should do. "If you need to take him home to nurse him . . ." I began.

"Didn't help Codrin, did it?"

That shut me up. I watched her cooking, her gnarled fingers moving with great precision. She tossed a pinch of salt into the pot, and I remembered the line in the stable. "Did you put that salt down in front of the door?"

"Thought it might help, but it didn't. Maybe nothing helps, once she's got your breath in her lungs."

"She?" I asked.

The Widow glared at me. "The *moroi*, fool child. Look!"

She turned and stalked out of the kitchen, snatching a knife up as she went. I followed warily, wondering if she planned to take me outside and stab me and what on earth I would do if she did.

Probably I would have to fire her for that. *Dammit.* Maybe it would be easier just to stay inside and avoid being stabbed.

I dithered in the doorway, but she turned and shot me a look full of irritated exhaustion shading into disappointment. I would rather have been stabbed than endure that look for long. I followed.

To my surprise, she made her way up the hill to the

springhouse. She moved slowly and I tried to offer her my arm, which went about like you would expect.

"Here," she said, standing at the entrance. She pointed to the side where the water no longer moved. "Here's where the moroi lives." She paused, then added grudgingly, "I think."

I looked dubiously at the springhouse. It was just a little stone structure, barely larger than a hut. "Where?"

"In the middle, you daft fool." She thumped her foot on the ground.

"You think there's someone buried in the middle?" I stared at the packed-earth floor. A body could be buried there, I suppose, if it was not particularly tall, or if it was doubled up. It wouldn't be a terribly smart place to bury a body, mind you, given the damp and presumably the smell, but it was at least technically feasible. And it's a hunting lodge, so if you buried someone right at the end of the season, you'd get most of a year before people came back and started asking questions like "Why does the springhouse smell like a corpse?"

The Widow nodded to me. "So my grandmother said, a time or two."

I rubbed my forehead. "But we've owned this place for years. Nobody ever had any problems. Why now?"

"Water stopped flowing," she said, pointing. "Keeps things in, doesn't it? Running water, even if it's just a trickle. That'd be why you bury someone in a springhouse, if you think they'll make trouble. But that rock fell and she got out."

"So you think someone buried her here to keep her contained." I rubbed the back of my neck. "But that's ridiculous. I'd have heard about it. Wouldn't I?"

She looked up at the sky and closed her eyes briefly, as if even God would have trouble believing the depths of my ignorance. "You think every body put in the ground gets recorded?"

"Well, no, obviously not, but . . ." I trailed off. What had the priest said? The spirits of those buried in unconsecrated ground? Yes, all right, I was being foolish. God knows we put enough bodies in the ground in the war without records, and it wasn't as if anyone was going to tell a child that there was a body in the springhouse. "Do you know who it is?"

The Widow shook her head. "Before my time," she said. "Before my grandmother's time, even. Just that someone was buried here. My grandmother said she heard tell it was a werewolf. I'd nearly forgotten, but when Codrin died . . . well. Doesn't take much to put it all together after that."

"But if you actually thought there was a moroi here, why did you take the . . ."

I stopped. The Widow stared fixedly at the entrance to the springhouse, her fists knotted in her apron, the gnarled fingers like clutching tree roots. Of course I knew why. She needed the money. She wasn't any braver than anyone else in the village, simply more desperate.

"Might have been wrong. Or she might not have taken anyone," she said shortly. "Might have taken you, or your man, or that nice foreign lady. Not that I *wanted* her to," she added, and that was probably true, although I doubt she'd have mourned much for me. *Young wastrel and general bad Gallacian gets what's coming to kan.*

"Oh," I said, because I didn't know what else to say.

"Should have known," the Widow said, more to herself than to me. "I'd have fought her. You or your man, you're soldiers. You'd fight. But my poor Bors, he never raised a hand in anger in his life." She gazed into the springhouse, but clearly she wasn't seeing it. "He was never any trouble. Even as a baby, he never fussed . . ."

She snapped back to herself, nodded sharply to me, and turned to make her way down the hill alone. I watched her go, looking from the dark springhouse to the old woman and back again, wondering what the hell to do next.

Christ's blood. I raked my hand through my hair. A *ghost, really?*

It's not that I'm a skeptic, you understand. It's just . . . look, so far as I'm concerned, ghosts are rather like ostriches.

("But Easton," you say, "*ostriches*? Really?" Hush, I'm getting to that.)

I don't doubt that ostriches exist. Many people who are far more intelligent than I am have traveled to the lands where ostriches dwell and reported back on their existence. There are photographs and taxidermy and centuries' worth of anecdotes and whole civilizations local to the ostrich who have produced great quantities of art depicting this noble bird.

Nevertheless, I *personally* have never seen an ostrich.

They simply don't play a large part in my life. If I woke in the night and heard footsteps in the hall, I would not immediately assume it was an ostrich. Why would I? Ostriches are things that happen to other people, far away, in countries more Serengeti-adjacent. If you want to tell me your saga of your encounter with an ostrich, I will listen appreciatively, but it's just not something I worry about happening to *me*.

Likewise, ghosts do not play any significant role in my life. I have slept in reputedly haunted houses and never seen anything worse than a stray cockroach. The howls of banshees and Gray Ladies fall on deaf ears (or at least ears rather badly affected by tinnitus). I've never attended a séance and while I have a vague skepticism about mediums, it's the same kind that I have about landlords and minstrels. Undoubtedly some of them are fine people, and I do not question the existence of either rental properties or music.

And before you say anything about Madeline Usher, she wasn't a ghost. What happened in that house on the edge of the tarn was unspeakably awful, but there was nothing supernatural about it. Nature creates horrors enough all by itself.

Nevertheless, here we were, and even if I didn't quite believe in the moroi, the Widow did. She seemed to think that the moroi was out and about because the springhouse was no longer containing her. I couldn't do much about Bors, but I could probably move that damn rock that had stopped the water flowing. Sure, it was heavier than I could lift on my own, but

I had brains and rope and a horse and probably between the three, I could get the water flowing again.

Hob did not appreciate being used to pull things. I explained to him that it was just a small rock and he explained to me that he was not a draft horse. After the application of treats, obscenities, and eventually outright begging, Angus arrived and oversaw the movement of the rock while I led Hob forward and told him that he was a good and faithful steed and also that if he stopped walking, I was going to let the Widow make paprika sausage out of him.

At last the rock turned sideways and got into the wider part of the channel. Water began to trickle sluggishly past the dam of mud that had built up around it. I dug into it with my hands, feeling them burn with cold, throwing muck to each side like a dog digging, until the trickle turned to a steady stream.

Sweating and cold is my least favorite combination. I wiped at my forehead with my sleeve, probably smearing mud across it. Angus, who had been holding Hob and watching this with bemusement, finally asked if there was any reason I'd chosen the coldest morning so far to engage in targeted demolitions.

"The Widow thinks the moroi lives in the springhouse."

Angus digested this for a moment. "And it can't cross running water, I suppose?"

"That seems to be the general idea." I looked at the ankle-deep flow, which didn't look as if it would slow a rabbit, let alone a ghost, then sighed and began leading Hob back to the stable.

Miss Potter emerged from the lodge in her immaculate walking dress and extremely sensible boots. I lifted a hand in greeting, aware that I looked neither immaculate nor sensible at the moment.

"Don't mind us," I said. "Just dealing with ghosts."

She digested this for a moment, then glanced up at the sky. "Nice weather for it," she observed.

I had to laugh. "I know, I know. You don't believe a word of it. I don't blame you, I'm not sure I do either."

Miss Potter gave me a surprisingly stern look. "You are making assumptions, Lieutenant, that are unfounded."

"Are you saying that you believe in ghosts?" I raised my eyebrows. Despite my personal view on the existence of ghosts, I had expected Miss Potter to be far more skeptical. "But you're a scientist."

"I am a *mycologist*, Lieutenant." She tapped my shin with her umbrella. "My intimate knowledge of fungi does not translate to a knowledge of spiritualism or souls or life after death. I loathe people who assume that because they are an expert in one field, they are therefore infallible on a totally unrelated topic, merely because they gave it five minutes of thought."

"Ah . . . hmm," I said. "So you think it *could* be a ghost?"

"It may be. I have no personal experience with such things myself." Miss Potter nibbled on her lower lip. "Proof would be required, however, and quite solid proof. Spiritualism was all the rage when I was a girl, but the press has reported many frauds as well."

I tried to imagine the Widow Botezatu perpetrating a table-rapping hoax and couldn't. And if she was trying to extort money from me, she was certainly going about it strangely. If nothing else, I believed that she believed. "I don't think it's a fraud. I just . . . ghosts? Really?"

"I've seen things," said Angus unexpectedly. "So have you, even if you won't admit it."

"I have *not*," I said, affronted.

He fixed me with a gimlet eye. "You never saw anything strange out at the front?"

I grimaced. "Sure I did, but that doesn't mean they were *real*. Things get weird and blurry after a few days, sure, but that doesn't mean it's *ghosts*."

"And you never heard a story that made you think twice?"

I opened my mouth, then closed it again. Because of course I had, hadn't I?

You hear a lot of stories from the line. Most of them are bullshit. You can usually tell because those are the ones that are all about ghosts and miracles and the Blessed Virgin putting Her hand in the way of a shell. They're *tidy*. They wrap everything up in a neat little bow, complete with punch line.

The ones you believe are the ones that aren't tidy. The ones that make no sense. Like one that Birdy told me, about the shepherd's hut. There was nobody alive in that hut, ka told me. It was one room and there was nowhere to hide. Birdy had shoulders like an ox and an imagination to match, and ka walked through that hut and walked out again, and swore on the grave of kan grandmother that it took an hour to cross that bare floor and someone sang lullabies the entire time. I believed it. I've never seen anyone so embarrassed to make a report and so determined to speak the truth anyway. You want to say that it was battle nerves or soldier's heart, go ahead if it makes you feel better. There are too many stories like that and people are embarrassed to tell them.

Angus cleared his throat and said, "World's a big place. I figure some bits just get overlooked sometimes. Like God goes around sweeping things up but He misses a corner now and again."

"That's technically blasphemy, Angus," I said mildly.

Angus uttered a nontechnical blasphemy, then flushed, remembering Miss Potter's presence. She hastily turned the corners of her lips down to hide her smile. I shook my head and set to work rubbing down my horse, to apologize for the work I'd made him do on a chilly autumn day.

It was cold and gray outside, and cool and dim inside the stable. I lit a lantern so that I could see what I was doing. Tiny gnats and pale moths came to circle the light and sear themselves against the glass.

Hob eventually forgave me, but it took some time. and when I rubbed his nose and told him that he was a good, handsome fellow, I realized that the silence had returned and settled like an unwelcome guest.

11

My body ached when I got up the next morning, and there was a thin glaze of ice across the puddles in the stableyard. I made certain that the horses had water, then staggered into the kitchen for coffee. My shoulder—the one that took an antique musket ball a few years back—felt as if someone had jammed a live coal into the socket.

"'Tis the wages of sin for drinking to excess," the Widow Botezatu suggested to God, slamming the teacup down on the table in front of me. "Some young wastrels think they can carouse to all hours and pay no price. But You and I know better, eh?"

"For you and God's information," I said, "I have not drunk a drop. I am paying the price for having moved that damn rock in the springhouse."

The silence that greeted this was so sudden and so profound

that for a moment it felt as if the terrible quiet of the woods had rushed into the room and drowned out the sounds of cooking.

"You moved the stone," the Widow said slowly.

"Yes?" I rubbed my forehead. Christ's blood, but I was tired. Sleeping in the stables was hard on a body. I had to remember that I wasn't twenty-five anymore. "The water's flowing again. I know you were worried about it."

"You thrice-damned young fool." She said it in the exact same tone that she said everything else, and for a moment it didn't even register as an insult. "Are you daft? Were you raised by hens? Did your mother nurse you on livrit? *Why would you do that?!*"

I hadn't expected her to throw herself on my neck in gratitude, but this did seem like a bit much. "Errr . . . but you said . . . ?"

"I said, but I don't know for certain. But you changed *something*, and now we'll find out more than we'd like . . . and Bors is *asleep!*" She flung down the fork at that last and sprinted for the stairs.

I would not have said that the Widow could run, but she put on a turn of speed that would have shamed a woman thirty years her junior. She had flung the door to the bedroom open before I had even reached the top of the steps. "*Bors!*"

I could hear the sounds before I reached the doorway. Bors was sitting up in bed, his eyes wide and sightless, making the short "*hk! hk! hk!*" sounds of a man whose lungs no longer draw in enough air. He pawed at the blankets, but I don't think he was awake.

The Widow, without so much as a pause, snatched the ewer of water from the bedside and dumped it over his head.

Bors came awake with a long, sucking breath, like a drowning man. He fell back against the pillows, clutching his chest, and for a moment it seemed like he had forgotten how to exhale, or that he was afraid that if he let the breath out, he would never get another.

"Child," said the Widow, wrapping her arms around his head. "Oh, my child, my love, my last one . . ."

I looked away, embarrassed. The Widow would have hated the thought of me witnessing some emotion from her other than exasperation.

"It was her, Nana," said Bors finally, his voice a croak. "It was the woman with the broken face."

"I know," said the Widow. "I know. You have to fight her, child."

"But Nana, I'm dreaming when it happens. I don't remember to fight her. I don't remember to do anything. It's a *dream*."

"I know." She lifted her head and looked at me with eyes like a person three days dead. "I know."

*

I waited in the kitchen, baffled and ashamed and more than a little alarmed. She came back down the steps, picked up the toasting fork, and for a minute I thought she actually was going to try to stab me. She settled for savagely impaling the toast instead.

"Is Bors . . . ?"

"No thanks to you," she growled. "You moved the stone, you fool."

This was far too complicated for me. "Uh . . . was that bad?"

"Yes, it's bad! Why do you think I didn't do it myself?"

What I actually thought was that she couldn't possibly have moved that rock herself, but it did not seem like the moment to point that out.

The Widow set down the fork, picked it up again, set it down, rattled the salt and pepper shakers, and then let out a long hiss of breath between her teeth. "Listen. Perhaps before she steals breath at night, yes? But maybe she knots the horse's tail, or goes calling with the owls instead. Maybe she blights the seed in the ground or the egg in the nest, then goes back to her body to sleep."

"Okay?"

"Soldiers," she said, with withering contempt. "You understand *nothing*. Do you know the birth cord?"

"Yes?" I assumed she was talking about the umbilical cord, although what that had to do with Bors, I couldn't begin to guess. In some parts of the country, people save it in a pouch to wear around the neck, although that always struck me as a bit squishy.

"You cut the cord, and the baby is on its own." She picked up a knife and slammed it down into the cutting board by way of explanation. I took a step back, wondering if I was genuinely going to have to defend myself. "No more food from mother, no more breath, no more warm place."

"Okay . . . ?"

"You cut the cord. You put the running water between the moroi and her body. No more food, no more breath, nowhere to sleep. Now she lives only in dreams. The dreams of my Bors."

"Um," I said. "I could put the rock back?"

I did not think it was possible for her to get angrier. She reached out and grabbed the front of my shirt in her fist and pulled me down. She was as strong as old tree roots and the lines of her face were etched as deeply as river gorges. "If you cut a rope, can you uncut it? You fool, you utterly useless fool. *Damn you*. And damn me twice for bringing my grandson here."

What was it about this ancient woman, as bent and worn as the mountains around us, that broke me so? "Just tell me what I was supposed to do," I begged. "Anything. Tell me how to fix this."

She pulled me down even farther, until we were nose to nose. The slight cloudiness of her eyes only made them look glazed with frost.

"Some things cannot be fixed," she hissed, and shoved me away.

She went back up to sit with Bors. Did she intend to stay awake all night, dumping water over his head whenever he stopped breathing?

What else can she do? She has no other choice, does she?

This is impossible, I argued with myself. *This cannot truly be happening.*

I sat at the table with my head in my hands, not knowing what to do next. Angus came in from settling the horses and looked at me inquiringly, and I seized on his help with relief. "Maybe you can make some sense of this muddle, Angus, because damned if I can."

He listened, nodded, then rubbed the back of his neck. "Hmm."

"How do I fix this?"

"I doubt you do. She's convinced it's the moroi, and it seems she's convinced Bors. Let them go back home until he's better."

"What if he doesn't *get* better?"

Angus sighed. "Then he will be like a thousand others in Gallacia this winter. The only difference is that you know his name."

"That doesn't make me feel any better."

"It wasn't meant to." He squeezed my shoulder in passing and went to go make dinner, since it was obvious that the Widow would not be cooking tonight.

That evening, fortified with livrit, I went upstairs to tell the Widow that she should take Bors home, and not to worry about the wages. I didn't get any farther than the door when I heard the Widow's voice.

For a moment I thought she was praying, and paused, not wanting to disturb her.

"Lady," came the voice through the door. "Lady Moroi, please don't take him."

Ah.

I looked down. Salt made a thick line across the threshold.

"He's a good boy," the Widow said. "He's the only blood an old woman's got left. I'm begging you, Lady, take one of the others. Take the soldier. Ka's a young fool, good for nothing but shooting other young fools. It was kan that set the water flowing around your body. Take kan instead. But leave me my grandson, who never did anyone any harm."

Well. It wasn't as if I expected any differently, but it still stung. And it was late, and it wasn't as if I could get the wagon tonight anyway.

I turned and crept back down the stairs, back to the stable and my own cold bed.

I saw the moth come in this time. It circled the room, a small white spark in the darkness, before finally landing on my chest. The weight of it was negligible at first, but it grew and grew and I tried to lift my hands to brush it away, but they were pinned beneath the blankets and the woman looking down at me had her hands on my shoulders, holding me in place.

"It's you again," I said, my voice weak in my ears. Speaking took breath and it was hard to draw more in to replace it. She was so heavy, or perhaps the moth was heavy and she was light.

(And yes, I knew this time that she was the moroi. I'm not an utter fool, though I realize that it's hard to tell sometimes. But Bors had been right. It was a *dream*. It was hard to feel any urgency. Everything was languid and slow. If I had been able to move, I might have fought her, or I might have danced a Viennese waltz with her. It hardly seemed to matter.)

"I moved the rock," I said, or thought I said.

She nodded.

"I wasn't supposed to, was I?"

The moroi shook her head. I began to apologize, but she gazed down at me with that slight, sad smile, and stroked her hand across my cheek.

Then her face tore apart.

12

It was as if her skin was a canvas and someone had ripped the bottom half loose. Her lips, still smiling, slid downward, along with her chin and half her cheeks. Rags of bloodless skin curled back, revealing emptiness. I stared up into her skull, into a hollow cavern of bone that seemed to fill her entire face, the inside red and ridged and damp.

There had been a Russian man named Peter who had taken a bullet to the back of the head. He was talking to me at the time, and for a split second, before he fell, I thought his face had looked a little like that. But I saw it for far less than a heartbeat and it had been clouded by a spray of blood and bone, and so I told myself that I could not have really seen it, that it was only another hideous image stitched together out of so many others.

The moroi inhaled and pulled the breath from my lungs.

It was not like a weight on my chest this time. It was like

having the air wrenched out of me. My breath suddenly had weight and form and it ripped at the soft tissues of my throat as she pulled it loose. Reflexively I clamped my mouth shut, but that only pulled the air out through my nostrils in agonizing streams.

I had faced so many deaths that I could no longer count them, but this one seemed so much worse than a bullet or a shell. "*Stop!*" I begged, and the word *stop* came out of my windpipe like a shard of glass, trailing blood and torn edges, to vanish into that empty cavern of skull.

Still she kept inhaling, until it seemed like there could not be a drop of air left in me, until my lungs must surely turn themselves inside out and fight their way up through my mouth in raw red chunks.

At last, she stopped.

I gasped in air and it hurt like nothing I'd ever felt before, more than the ball in my shoulder had hurt, pain so brutal that I tried to stop breathing, but my body had the reflexes of the nearly drowned and kept pulling the air back in, even as I choked and spasmed and clawed at the sheets.

The moroi sat back. I could still see her smile, dangling loosely on the rag of flesh below her skull. The hollow of her head shifted slightly. It was far too dark, more like a railway tunnel than a human throat. Her fingers were cool as she stroked my cheek, and the sad, hopeful look in her eyes never changed.

"No more," I croaked, my mouth tasting of bile and copper. "Please."

She shook her head. The lower half of her face swayed back and forth, the curve of the smile trembling like a leaf in an autumn wind.

And then she leaned forward and inhaled again, and I learned that it was possible to lose consciousness in a dream.

When I woke, at first, I couldn't move. My chest felt like a pane of shattered glass. I focused on breathing, which hurt, and then I tried not breathing, which was not sustainable in the long term. Eventually I settled on breathing very shallowly through my mouth. My lungs felt as if they were filled with concrete to just beneath my collarbone, leaving me with only the tiniest space in which to breathe.

What had I *done* to myself?

It was the moroi. You know it was the moroi.

It can't have been, I argued with myself, not with much conviction. *That was a dream. The moroi is nothing but a local superstition.*

My brain didn't even bother to reply. Dreams didn't do this to your lungs.

I could still be dreaming? Maybe?

I took another sip of air between raw lips and winced. I'd never known a dream could hurt so badly.

With some difficulty, I sat up. The room was dark, the open door a rectangle of lighter gray. There was still a handkerchief in the keyhole, for all the good it did when the door hung open. The air felt like ice, which had to be making everything worse.

If I can get to the lodge, it will be warmer and it probably won't hurt as much to breathe. If it was a dream, I would wake up eventually. If it wasn't, I had better get help or I might not wake up ever again.

If it's a dream, the moroi may still be here somewhere.

That settled it. If this was a dream and she was still here, then if I stayed here, she knew where to find me.

Getting to my feet took more heroism than most of the things they'd given me medals for. I had to crawl to the door and grab the doorknob to help haul myself up. Every single muscle along my ribs was an individual knot of agony.

Once I was upright, it was a little easier. I went down the line of stalls, holding on to the uprights. Eventually I was going to reach the stableyard and then I would have nothing to hang on to. I decided to worry about that once I got there.

Hob poked his nose over the top of the stall door and looked at me curiously. A thread of alarm went through me. It was so cold in the stable. The horses must be cold as well. I should do . . . something . . .

The notion of putting a blanket over Hob's back made me want to weep. I would have to twist and lift and raise my arms, and then I would probably collapse in his stall. Not that Hob would ever trample me, but he would certainly be alarmed.

I'll go inside and wake Angus. Angus can help the horses. Angus can help me.

I patted Hob's nose, meaning to be reassuring, and my

hand went inside him.

I think if it had simply passed through, like a mirage, I could have borne it. I would have been confused, but not appalled. It would not have been something I understood, but I have had a great deal of experience with things that I don't understand.

But it was not like that.

My fingers sank into his hide as if it were no thicker than a moth's wing, and plunged into something dry and spongy, which crumbled away from my touch. I yanked my hand back, too shocked to really comprehend what had happened, and great rags of skin came with it, sliding off Hob's skull as if they were barely anchored to the bone.

I could not scream, but I made a dreadful hoarse noise and stumbled backward. It was the first sound that I had heard since I woke and only then did I realize that the silence lay over everything like a coat of frost. I had not heard my own breathing or my own footsteps. I had heard nothing at all.

Hob swiveled his ears toward me when I cried out. Rather, he swiveled one ear. The other had fallen away, along with half his face. I was looking at his skull, just as I had looked at the moroi's skull in my dream. The dry spongy texture had been bone. I could see my fingermarks in it, above his exposed teeth, and as I watched, the bone crumbled into a fine dust that sifted down onto the ground at my feet.

He did not seem to be in pain. He did not seem even to have noticed. I tore my eyes away and looked down at my hand, at the rags of flesh that clung to my wrist as weightlessly as the dust of a moth's wings, that had torn apart just as the moroi's face had. Bay and black hairs and a fine pointed ear, and in the center, a dark, mild eye that swiveled and looked up at me, despite having neither socket or muscle behind it.

My scream was louder this time, and I barely noticed how much it hurt, or how the silence smothered it. I slammed my hand against the stall, trying to shake the horrible living skin away. I couldn't bear to touch it with my other hand. I scraped it against the wood instead, whimpering as Hob's face fell away from my fingers in reluctant fragments.

"Hob," I croaked, looking up. "Oh God, Hob—"

The long bones of his skull were honeycombed with rot. He twitched his ear again and then he simply fell apart, his skin collapsing to the bottom of the stall like a rotten puffball. Moths fluttered outward on wings paler than bone. I saw a little cloud of dust rise and thought, *Spores*, and the terror of that, of anything fungal coming for someone I loved, was enough to drive me staggering forward.

I was blind with tears and had forgotten that Angus's gelding was in the next stall. He shoved my shoulder with his nose, and I shrieked. It was like being poked with a rotting log that crumbles even as it touches you. *Don't look*, I thought, *don't look*. I'd learned long ago that things you don't see can kill you, but at least the visions don't stalk your mind for decades after.

I didn't look into the stall, but something waved at the

edge of my vision, something on me, and I looked down involuntarily. Long, desiccated strips that fluttered like bunting from my upper arm. I scraped them off against the wall. More moths filled the air, battering against my face. One brushed my lips as if it was seeking the darkness inside. When I slapped it away, shreds of horsehide clung to my face. My stomach clenched but if I vomited through my broken throat, I really would die.

This has to be a dream. It has to be. Wake up, wake up,
WAKE UP!

But I didn't. And if it was a dream, then the moroi could find me.

When I reached the door, outlined in cracks of moonlight, I almost cried again. My hand still seemed to be working, despite what it had touched. I supposed that was good. I could cut it off later. I lifted the latch and pushed it open.

The moon blazed blue and silver across the stableyard, turning it into an alien landscape. The house was hundreds of miles away. A faint yellow glow crept around the edge of one set of shutters. Someone was sitting up with a candle. Maybe it was Angus. Maybe he could tell me what had happened to the horses, if only I could reach him.

I set my eyes on the door and began to walk.

It took years. The moon beat down while I crept as slowly as a beetle across the infinity of the yard. My tears froze on my cheeks and the air stabbed my lungs like a knife, no matter how shallowly I breathed. I had to detour around the wood-splitting stump and that added hours to my journey. I truly think that if I had not experienced forced marches, I would not have made it. They would have found my frozen body in the morning and the Widow would talk to God about young fools who could do nothing right, not even walk across a stableyard.

When I finally reached the door, I barely believed it. I had been walking forever. Walking was all I did. My skin was numb and I could not feel my feet. That was fine. I could cut them off later, too.

It took both hands, barely working together, to open the door. I nearly fell inside, but caught myself on the doorframe. Warm air struck me like a blow and I swayed on my feet.

I will not faint. I will get Angus.

I tried to call his name. It came out as a moan, pathetically thin, swallowed up immediately by the silence. He could not have heard that from across the room, let alone upstairs.

I licked my lips and tried again. The silence laughed at my feeble efforts.

It occurred to me that if the moroi was here, I would not hear her coming.

Antlers gleamed in the watery moonlight. The thread that bound them was brilliant red, the color that blood doesn't stay for long. I could see the color clearly despite the darkness, but I was in too much pain to find that strange. The boar grinned down at me, its tusks dirty yellow, wrapped in thread. It looked as if it had just gored someone. Perhaps that was what was wrong with my chest, I'd been gored.

Keep your head, Easton. Keep your head and get Angus.

No one could hear me shouting. No help for it. I went to the stairs.

I had to get each foot on the step before I could tackle the next, but I managed. My breath came a little easier now. It might have been the warmth, or that the cold had numbed the pain in my ribs. It might have been the last burst of energy before dying.

When I reached the hallway, I turned. Angus's door was ajar, and I praised the Blessed Virgin and the hundred little saints for that mercy. I pushed it open.

"Angus," I croaked. "*Angus.*" The silence grabbed the words as soon as they left my lips and spun them away into nothingness.

Angus was asleep on his side, heavy quilt pulled up to his chin. My hand hovered over his shoulder, but I paused. Angus has never shown any sign of soldier's heart, but poking an old soldier in their sleep is not terribly wise.

The pause gave me long enough to realize that I'd nearly done something terrible. What if I touched him and he fell apart, the same way that the horses had?

I could picture it far too clearly, his skin tearing away in strips, his body collapsing in on itself like overripe fruit. Moths crawling out from underneath, as if his skin was an old coat they'd been devouring from the inside. Would his face stick to my fingers too, mustache twitching, his eyes rolling to gaze up at me?

I pulled my hand back. "Angus," I said, again, pleading, and this time I might as well not have spoken at all and saved my battered throat the trouble.

He didn't move. I could see the rise and fall under the blankets, but I could hear nothing at all.

For lack of anything else to do, I turned away and limped down the hall toward my bedroom. I was so tired, and the warm glow of the candle was so inviting. Perhaps if I could lie down in my own bed for just a moment or two, I could get my wits back together.

I pushed open my bedroom door. The line of salt on the floor stung at my feet like nettles, but that was nothing compared to the pain in my chest.

Bors lay in my bed, shrouded with blankets, and the Widow sat in a chair beside him, the candle glowing beside her. I slumped in the doorway. Of course that was why I wasn't sleeping in my bed.

"Sorry," I said, reflexively. "I forgot."

Not that she could hear me . . . or could she?

For the Widow looked up almost immediately, her eyes scanning the room. They passed over me in the doorway, unseeing, and I realized, before I could even begin to hope, that she couldn't see me. She was reacting to the door having opened, nothing more.

Perhaps this wasn't a dream. Perhaps I had died and I was a ghost. Served me right for having thought that they would never have anything to do with me.

Christ's blood, if that's true, why does it still hurt so much? It would be just my luck, to be a ghost who could still open doors and feel pain.

"Who's there?" the Widow asked sharply. Her words cut through the deadly silence, sharp as swords. "Is someone . . . *oh.*" She caught herself, and I dared to hope that she might have realized that I was there.

"It's me," I said. "It's Easton." The words resonated inside my skull, the way that speech always does, bouncing between the bones of my jaw and my ear, but that was all. The silence snatched them away.

"It's you," said the Widow. She reached out to the nightstand and picked something up, holding it tightly in her fist.

Could she hear me? "Yes, it's me."

"I know you've come for his breath," she said, looking past me. "I know you want to finish what you've started. I'm begging you, Lady Moroi, to take someone else."

"No," I said futilely, "I'm not the moroi. I'm Easton. *Easton.*"

"Lady," she said, holding up the object in her hand. It was a pair of scissors, partly open, with the handles tightly bound in red thread. "Lady Moroi. I offer you a bargain. I am old and there isn't much breath left in me, but I will give it to you freely, if you promise to take the soldier and spare my Bors."

"Widow Botezatu," I said, taking a step forward. "I know you hate me, but I'm not the moroi. I'm Easton."

"I'm sorry, sir," Bors said mournfully beside me. "She can't see me, either."

I jerked sideways, startled, and fell against the doorframe, pushing the door farther open. It seemed as if the Widow ought to notice the door moving, but her eyes remained fixed on nothing, the scissors held up before her like a crucifix.

Bors leaned against the wall beside the door. He looked the same as he always did, his arms folded tightly across his chest as if to keep his breath in.

"Bors? You're awake?"

He gave this matter due consideration. "I don't think so. Are you awake?"

"I don't know anymore." It didn't feel like a dream. There was nothing slow or languid about it. But if it was a dream, maybe the horses hadn't torn into mothwing shreds and stuck to my hands. Maybe the moroi was only a creature of the dream. Maybe I could wake up.

"Are we really talking?" I asked Bors. "Or am I only dreaming I'm talking to you?"

Bors frowned, clearly working through this one. I realized that I had just posed him one of the classic philosophical conundrums of history, minus the bit about butterflies, and held up a hand to forestall it. "Don't worry about it."

The Widow, still holding the thread-wrapped scissors in front of her, turned her head back and forth. "Lady Moroi? If you are there, give me a sign. Accept my bargain, I beg of you."

"I wish she wouldn't do that," said Bors sadly. "I don't want the moroi to take her breath, or yours. It isn't right."

"Well, no. But she does it because she loves you, not . . ." I trailed off. The Widow had moved the scissors, and something winked briefly in the light.

Caught between the blades was a strand of sandy blond hair. I knew that color well, because I saw it often enough in my mirror.

The Widow untangling stray hairs from my brush, clucking her tongue, as she harangued me about attending church. She hadn't even tried to hide it. That was what galled me. She had tucked them away, right in front of me, and I had watched her do it and never thought twice about it. It was only a couple of hairs, nothing but trash to be cleaned away.

"Take the soldier," the Widow said, her voice far too close to a prayer. "I've made it easy for you. Cut the soldier's life, not my Bors!" And she snapped the scissors closed with a cold metallic sound.

Severed halves of a single hair drifted downward. Some sixth sense chilled down my spine and the silence thickened and deepened until I could barely hear the words in my own throat.

The moroi was close. I could feel her. I looked over my shoulder, down the hall, and saw nothing. Would I see her coming? Was there a sign that she was close?

Bors moaned softly, putting his hands over his face, and I was sure he felt it too. The Widow stilled, her eyes narrowing to slits. Her knuckles went white around the scissors. On the bed, the blankets moved.

On the bed.

"Bors," I said, "if you're here, then who's—"

The moroi sat up. Her skull was still a gaping ruin of bone and darkness. The skin of her face lay against her chest, still smiling at nothing. She looked from me to Bors, then at the old woman sitting at her bedside, holding the scissors like a talisman.

She reached toward the Widow, and I lunged.

I would like to say that it was calculated, that I knew that the Widow did not love me but that I had chosen to be the bigger person. Something like that. Something noble and self-sacrificing. But it wasn't. I saw an enemy grabbing at someone unaware of their presence, and reflex took over. I barreled forward, slamming into the chair between them.

The moroi's eyes, still human, went wide. I waited for her to grab me, but somehow Widow Botezatu was faster. She lashed out, quick as a snake, striking at thin air with the scissors. I flung up my hands reflexively and a steel blade nicked my palm and I fell down,

down

down

and landed in three inches of mud just inside the Bulgarian border.

13

I drew in a great sucking breath in surprise and that hurt so badly that I thumped my fist against the ground, trying to drive the pain away. Sadly, that ground was also mud. *Squelch.* Droplets of muck showered over me. I wiped the mud from my face with my sleeve and stared up into a cold white sky framed by pine trees.

I knew exactly where I was, of course. The mountains on the way to Slivnitsa, a place I've been once in reality and hundreds of times in my dreams. The reason that my countrymen and I were here, because somebody needed to scout through the mountains and King Milan hadn't felt like calling up most of his own army for his trifling little war of aggression.

The generals swore that it would be clear and cold and we'd be fighting on dry grass at Slivnitsa, but of course it had been a slog of rain and snow and fog for two days. The mountains were colder and I was glad to have snow instead of rain, but if you put an army camp anywhere it generates mud around it.

For a minute, I thought about just staying there. It was cold and I was lying in mud, but in an hour or two, I would stop feeling cold and start feeling warm. Sure, I'd die, but I wouldn't kill any Bulgarians in the process, which would be a good thing. Milan could go fuck himself sideways.

I took another breath. This one hurt less. Maybe it wouldn't take an hour after all.

"Sir," Birdy said urgently, "get up."

I tilted my head. Birdy was standing over me, looking about how I felt, except slightly less muddy.

"I can see up your nose," I informed kan.

"Sir, we've got to go *now*."

"Yes, of course." Birdy reached down and pulled me to my feet before it occurred to me to worry that ka would tear apart into mothwing rags at my touch. But ka didn't, and I breathed a sigh of relief, which still hurt, but not as much. Maybe my lungs were healing? No, that couldn't be, lungs take forever and the moroi had just . . . it had only been a few minutes . . . but no, we'd been in the mountains for days, hadn't we?

I shook my head to clear it. "This is a dream," I muttered. It had to be—but there was mud in my left boot and sliding in chilly globs down the back of my neck and I could not remember any dream that had ever so exactly replicated that sensation.

"It's a goddamn nightmare is what it is," said Birdy. "What are your orders?"

I wiped at my neck, looking around. "Where are the horses?" But as soon as I said it, I remembered—the horses had been scattered and we had to go find them. Right. I had lived this already. "That way," I said, pointing. "They didn't go far."

Birdy nodded, pulling kan revolver. I did the same, checking it for mud. I wanted to stop and clean it because who knew how long it had been since I cleaned it? A week or last night or eight years or . . . I stared down at the gun. Gasser M1870, which told me nothing at all. I'd been using one of those practically since I shaved my head and joined the army. Gallacia bought the things by the wagonload from Austria. (Heh. My drill sergeant had sworn that by the time we were done, we'd be able to take one apart in our sleep. I could actually find out if that was true.)

"Sir?"

Right. Birdy was waiting. I set out. The mud and the snow had combined into a nasty muck, but as we got farther away from the camp—*What camp? Where was the camp? Shouldn't the camp be behind me?*—it solidified into frozen muck, which was nasty in a different way. I could see hoofprints in it.

Looking over my shoulder to where the camp should be, I saw only trees. "Birdy, where's the camp?" I asked.

Birdy didn't answer. Birdy wasn't there. A moth lay on the ground where ka had stood, frozen and unable to rise. It batted its wings once, twice, then lay still.

I turned in a circle and realized that I was alone in the woods. Silence washed over me, deeper and colder than the snowfall. I closed my eyes for a single despairing heartbeat. The moroi had followed me here.

If I can get to my horse, maybe I can get away. Skipper had to be around here somewhere. If I could find him, I could rely on his senses instead of my own feeble human ones.

I followed the hoofprints. I could feel the moroi behind me, like a soundless weight. Sometimes I would get far enough ahead that I could hear snow and pine needles crunching underfoot, but then the silence would brush against me again.

The footing was better here. Not as muddy, anyway. This ground had not been churned up by the passage of boots or hooves. As soon as I noticed that, I realized that there were no hoofprints in front of me, and when I turned, there were none behind me either. *Christ's blood.* Where had my horse gone? I was useless without him. He was the one who had spotted the Bulgarian hiding in the trees two days ago and I'd retreated down the trail and both of us had lived to fight another day. Or all three of us, I suppose, if you count Skipper.

Skipper died years ago, whispered the part of my brain that reminds me that I'm not in the war. *This is a dream.*

"Shows what you know," I muttered. "Maybe you're the bit that's dreaming."

I lost the last words as the silence covered me. The moroi was gaining.

I caught occasional glimpses of her now. She flitted from tree to tree, hiding herself behind the dark pine boughs. Sometimes when she touched a branch, it unraveled, falling apart into skeins of bark and shadow that pooled atop on the snow. Sometimes as snow fell from the trees, it grew mothwings and flew.

It occurred to me that if I could make it above the tree line, she would have nowhere to hide.

And what good will that do me? I'll see my death coming a little farther off?

Besides, if I went that far up, I'd be a sitting duck for any Bulgarians who wanted to take a shot at me.

Heh. Maybe I'll get lucky and they'll shoot the moroi instead.

My thoughts stuttered to a halt and I had to stop and back them up, like a balked horse.

I was dreaming, and the moroi was in my dream. And I was in the war. Could I fight her here?

You have to fight her, the Widow had told Bors. And he'd said that he couldn't because it was a dream and he couldn't remember. That made sense. Bors would never fight anyone. But I was a soldier, for my sins, and I had fought people who deserved it far, far less than the moroi.

It couldn't be that simple. What happens in dreams doesn't happen in reality. I know that they say if you die in a dream, you die in your sleep, but how often does that actually happen? People would be dropping like flies.

But the moroi had been stealing Bors's breath in a dream, and it had been real. And she'd stolen Codrin's breath, too. Village gossip had been right, and his daughter and I had been wrong.

That can't be true. Someone has to have fought back before.

Maybe they had. Maybe they'd fought and driven her back to her body and then killed her and buried her in the springhouse. It had all happened at least a century ago, before the Widow's grandmother's time. Long enough ago that it had gotten mixed up with stories of werewolves and ghosts. Long enough that the Widow didn't know how to fight her and had been reduced to putting up every ward from every old fairy tale she knew. She could have had a hundred victims then, or a half dozen. Or maybe she hadn't been a moroi at all, she'd just been a woman who was in the wrong place at the wrong time and someone murdered her and buried her in unconsecrated ground, and she found herself walking in Codrin's dreams.

"Blessed Virgin," I whispered, even though I couldn't even hear myself. "Why must you keep sending me innocent monsters?"

I had stopped walking. I stood in a little clearing in the pines. The snow had drifted deeper around their edges, as snow does.

The moroi stepped out from behind a tree and faced me. Her face had slid down to her chest and lay in folds like a scarf. Soft gray eyes gazed at me over that sucking gray cavern of bone.

"Did someone murder you?" I asked her. "Are you just confused?"

Those eyes blinked but she made no response. A halo of moths framed her like the icon of a lost saint.

This can't work, I thought, and pulled my revolver and fired.

The shot was so muffled that if not for the recoil and the sudden cloud of black smoke, I would not have known that I fired. But the Austrian gunsmiths knew their work and the gun went off and the moroi screamed and part of her side was torn to white rags and the air was suddenly like glue and she was on top of me and I went down.

I thrashed but she was as heavy as guilt. The moroi pinned my shoulders with both hands and bent over me. I saw the cavernous tunnels of her true face, inches away from my own, and tried to pull back, but only succeeded in smacking the back of my head against the ground. It might have been nice to lose consciousness again, but the snow hadn't packed hard enough to do that.

She breathed in and ripped my breath out of my throat for the third time. She pulled at me and it seemed like not just the air but the whole world should vanish inside her. First my lungs would unravel and then my heart and guts and bones, all of them turned to threads and dragged out through my mouth until I was left a hollowed-out husk.

My chest was a vise. I was going to die here in the snow and probably I deserved it. I had wanted to die earlier, hadn't I? The moroi wanted to live and to live she had to take my breath and for all I knew, she had lived a good and blameless life before she was murdered. You couldn't say the same for me, could you?

Spots bloomed in my vision. Pinpricks at first, but growing larger, not just black but jittery red and gold around the edges. My throat was a seamless sleeve of pain and the moroi kept inhaling. How had Bors not died outright? How had he endured this, night after night?

Bors.

Christ's blood. She was going to kill Bors, wasn't she? The Widow had tried to offer her a bargain, but the moroi wouldn't keep it. She would drink my breath and the Widow's and that wouldn't be enough. Maybe it would take a few days or weeks, but she'd come for Bors. She wouldn't be able to help herself. Maybe the world wouldn't mourn either of us, but Bors was innocent in all this.

My shoulders were pinned, but that didn't matter. I only had to bend my right elbow and pull the trigger.

The moroi screamed again. I saw the pulse of wet, ridged meat inside her skull as the scream came out, accompanied by a blast of wet air that had lately been inside my lungs. I inhaled desperately, our breaths mingling in horrid intimacy, and then I fired again and again, pulling the trigger long after the gun had run dry, until I slowly realized that I was hearing the clicks and the silence had stopped.

The moroi lay collapsed across my chest like a lover. Her

eyes were half-open, the pupils huge. *It can't have worked*, I thought. *You can't really kill someone in a dream.*

This isn't just a dream, though. It's the war.

I lay on my back and looked up into the cold gray sky. My lungs no longer wanted to move. The moroi's dead weight on my chest was still less than it had been before, but I could not imagine shifting it.

They tell you that everything gets dark at the end, but it went white instead, the color of snow falling outside a window, and all I had to do was sit and watch it fall, forever.

14

"Ka's waking up, I think," Miss Potter said. And then, louder, "Alex? Alex, can you hear me?"

I knew there was no point in answering, not with the silence muffling everything. Still, Miss Potter was talking to me, and that meant that either I was alive or we were both dead. I didn't have an opinion on which it might be. As long as I could go back to sleep, either was fine.

"Alex, if you can sit up, this will be much easier."

On second thought, I hoped that Miss Potter wasn't dead. That would make Angus sad. Of course, if she was alive, then I was probably alive, and that seemed implausible. The inside of my mouth tasted absolutely foul. Surely living mouths weren't allowed to taste like that.

Miss Potter said something I didn't quite catch. She sounded worried. I heard a low rumble in reply, and recognized Angus's voice. Perhaps all three of us were dead. That would be fine. Miss Potter could go to mycologist's heaven, where the Royal Society publishes papers by women, and Angus could go with her. I could stay here and sleep.

"Easton," said Angus, sounding a bit stern.

I would have liked to reassure him, but of course he wouldn't have been able to hear me. I could perhaps have done something in mime, but it seemed like so much work.

"*Easton, report!*"

I sat bolt upright in bed. I could have been cold in my coffin and I would have responded to that tone of voice. My eyes flew open. They stung, partly because of the sudden light, but also because my eyelids had been gummed shut and opening them yanked a dozen eyelashes free from their moorings.

Dead people probably don't care about their eyelashes. Also, dead people's heads probably don't hurt as much as mine suddenly did.

"Whuh—?" I said, and began coughing violently.

"Angus," said Miss Potter sternly, "that was *not* kind."

"Worked though, aye?"

A blurry, flesh-colored blob resolved into Miss Potter's face. "Lieutenant," she said, pushing me gently back against a pile of pillows. "Welcome back."

I drew a thin breath. It didn't hurt as much as it had in my dream. It still didn't feel *good*, but it went in, and then back out again. I could feel a cough lurking at the bottom of my lungs and tried to leave it there.

"Here," said Angus gruffly, holding a cup to my lips. It tasted foul, but strangely familiar. Actually, it tasted like the inside of my mouth, which probably meant that I'd been drinking it before.

"Whuh," I said again, a bit more coherently. "Whuh ha'ened . . . ?"

"You've had pneumonia," said Miss Potter. "The doctor's been here twice."

"Starting to think I should have just built that sauna," Angus added.

I tried another sip of the foul brew. Something medicinal, I guessed. The smell cleared my sinuses like a fox clears a henhouse. As long as it came from the doctor and not the Widow, that's all I asked.

It occurred to me that I wasn't wearing a night shirt. I was wearing a poultice of some sort, which smelled like death and camphor, but it did not provide much in the way of modesty. Granted, my breasts are fairly insignificant, but it was still a bit awkward, particularly with a very respectable Englishwoman at my bedside. I tried to cover myself with my hands. "Err," I said. "Could I . . . perhaps . . . ?"

"Of course," said Miss Potter smoothly, standing up. "I'll see about more tea."

Angus waited until she had left the room, then helped me into a shirt. I was strong enough to get my arm into one of the sleeves, but that left me too exhausted to tackle the other one. He pulled it on for me, while reading me several consecutive riot acts.

"Miss Potter saved your life, you blithering idiot. What the hell were you doing wandering around in your nightclothes?"

I blinked blearily at him. "I was what?"

"What the hell were you doing? Were you *drunk*?"

I shook my head to clear it, which was a tactical error. The room spun. I held my head and moaned weakly. When I could focus again, Miss Potter was back, holding a steaming tea tray.

"Angus," she said, "don't yell until ka's better."

The second cup was regular tea and it tasted like ambrosia. "My house and lands are yours," I promised Miss Potter extravagantly.

"I'm not sure I want them," she said. "This place at least seems unlucky."

The memory of my nightmare had faded somewhat, but her words brought it roaring back. I nearly dropped the teacup. "Bors!"

"Is fine, so far as I know," said Angus. "The priest says he's recovering better than you are. The Widow took him home three days ago."

"Three days . . . ?" I remembered that he said the doctor had been here twice. "How long have I been out?"

"I found you four days ago," said Miss Potter. "In the springhouse, of all places."

"*What?*"

She nodded. "Early in the morning. I realized I hadn't gotten a good spore print of the *Mycena* and thought I would go pick another one. Instead I found you in the middle of the floor, half in the water. I was afraid you'd drowned."

"You're damn lucky you didn't freeze to death," Angus growled. "You were colder than a wolf's arse-hai—" He remembered Miss Potter and cut off abruptly.

"Colder than a wolf's toes," said Miss Potter tranquilly. "What *were* you thinking, Lieutenant?"

"But I wasn't in the springhouse." I put my hand to my throbbing forehead. Tinnitus buzzed through me as I clenched my jaw, and I missed the next few words.

". . . certainly *were*."

"I came out of the stable and came straight here," I said slowly. "I remember it. The horses fell apart and then—oh God, the horses!" I tried to sit upright again, bent just wrong, and suffered another coughing fit.

"The horses are fine," said Angus, whacking me on the back. Something dislodged painfully and Miss Potter handed me a handkerchief, as if she listened to people hack their lungs up every day. I hope her country realized how perfect an example of Britishness she was. "Hob's a bit bored, that's all."

"Yes, of course . . ." I mumbled, sinking back. A thought struck me. "If the Widow's gone, though, what about . . . propriety?"

"Oh, *hang* propriety," said Miss Potter. Angus reached out and took her hand. I smiled, I think. I tried, anyway. Even my lips ached.

"Why were you worried about the horses?" asked Angus.

"It was just a dream I had. I was back in Bulgaria and the moroi was there . . ."

"Perhaps you were sleepwalking," said Miss Potter.

That made more sense than anything else. Pneumonia could lead to fever and hallucinations. Perhaps I had already been sickening, and my dream had been woven together to make sense of the pain in my chest and the cold and feverish stumble across the stableyard.

It was all very logical and very rational. I didn't believe a word of it. But I drank my medicine and let Angus rail at me, which is how Angus shows affection, and finally Miss Potter told him to stop pestering me and let me sleep.

I did not dream of either the moroi or the war.

*

"You're in no condition to do this," said Angus. "You should still be in bed."

"You're absolutely right," I said. "You take the shovel."

We stood in front of the springhouse a few days later. I was well enough to get out of bed, according to Dr. Virtanen if not Angus, though I was under strict orders not to overexert myself. I did feel much better, though Miss Potter was convinced that any exposed skin meant that I would re-sicken, so I was swathed in so many scarves and blankets that I looked like a brightly colored haystack.

I was fairly certain that I was not going to re-sicken. My

recovery had been almost preternaturally swift. Dr. Virtanen had put it down to clean living. I put it down to a lack of nocturnal visitors, but I wasn't going to tell him that.

Nevertheless, even if it no longer felt like my lungs had been attacked with a cheese grater, I was happy to have Angus do the heavy work of digging up the grave in the springhouse.

"You realize there may be nothing here," Angus said after tackling the hard earth for five minutes, making no appreciable dent, and coming back with a mattock.

I shrugged. I had told Angus some of it, late, over purely medicinal livrit. I don't know whether he believed me or not. On some level, I think I had hoped that he would tell me it was all in my head. But he didn't, and here we were.

It took a long time. The earth had been packed so hard that it was as dense as stone. The mattock eventually broke through the crust and it became shovel work again for a little while. I took as long a turn as Angus would allow, which wasn't much.

Hours later, we were only about two feet down and I was starting to doubt myself. What proof did I have that the moroi was buried here? The Widow's word, that was all, and that was based on little better than a rumor handed down from her grandmother. Was I driving Angus to exhaustion based on nothing more than a fever dream?

"Easton . . ." He sat back, looking at the pitifully small hole we'd dug. "Perhaps we can work on it more tomorrow?"

"Let me help," said Bors.

We both jumped. I had the excuse of convalescence, at least, but Angus nearly dropped the mattock.

"Bors?" I blinked at him. "I thought you were still sick!"

"No." He looked at me and nodded slowly, and I was sure, in that moment, that he was remembering standing in the bedroom, in a dream that wasn't quite a dream. "I recovered very quickly."

"I'm glad," I said. "But you shouldn't be . . ."

He took the mattock from Angus and swung it with the casual strength of a Gallacian youth who picks up the cattle when it's time to move them to the barn. Five quick chops and the hole was half again the size it had been.

"I loosened the dirt for him," muttered Angus.

"Uh-huh," I said.

It was less than twenty minutes later when the mattock hit something that wasn't dirt. Cloth, by the sound of it. Very old cloth, which fell apart almost as soon as we touched it. We shoveled away what we could, then began clearing dirt from the cloth with our hands.

Miss Potter came out and I thought she was going to yell at us—or at least me—for kneeling in the cold dirt, no matter how many scarves I was wearing. But she sighed and left and came back again with the oil lamps from the house, then rolled up her sleeves and knelt in the dirt alongside us.

"Eugenia—"

"If you attempt to tell me that I should not be digging out

of some misplaced gallantry, I shall strike you very hard with my
umbrella."

". . . yes'm."

(I translated this quietly for Bors, who laughed loudly, then
turned bright red. Miss Potter hummed to herself.)

"Is it a sack?" I asked, as we cleared more of the cloth.

"A cloak, I think," said Miss Potter. "See, here's the edge."
She delicately fitted her fingers under the dirt-encrusted cloth
and tried to peel it back.

It broke away in a stiff, scab-like chunk. Underneath, the
oil lamp gleamed on teeth and a pale crust of white and gray
curved in the rough shape of a cheek.

I sat back on my heels and let out a long, long sigh.

*

Angus and Bors wrapped up the moroi's body—what was left
of it—and promised to carry it to Father Sebastian. Miss Potter
bullied me back inside and made me drink hot tea, although
the British seem to think that it's better with milk. Still, Angus
was passionately in love with her, so I let it lie.

"Bors," I said, as Angus saddled the horses, "what made you
come out here? Not that I'm not glad you came."

If I was expecting some mystical connection to my quest to
excavate the moroi's bones, I was disappointed. "Left my good
axe," he explained. "And some clothes. I came to pick them up.
Grandmother . . . err . . ." He looked embarrassed.

"It's fine," I said. We both knew—at least, I was pretty sure that we both knew—that his grandmother had offered me to the moroi in his stead. Not even the indomitable Widow was willing to look me in the eye after that.

Which reminded me of something. "Wait just a moment. She left something here." I went upstairs, shedding scarves, and reached under the bed.

I had found the scissors there the day after I was allowed out of bed. The handles were still wrapped in red thread, though one side had nearly frayed through. I brushed away a strand of blond hair that had clung to the metal.

I didn't know what had happened that night after I jumped between the moroi and the Widow, and I was fairly certain that I would never find out, either. It happens that way sometimes. I found that I didn't actually care that much, either.

One of the points had a smear of dried blood across it. I wiped it off and handed them to Bors across my sleeve, handle first, like someone offering a sword.

"Thank you," said Bors. He looked as if he might say something else, then closed his mouth firmly and tucked them away.

"Give Father Sebastian my regards," I said, and finally yielded to Miss Potter's demands that I go lie down before I caught my death.

*

Angus took Miss Potter to the station three days later. I let them go alone in order to have a private goodbye. Before she left, though, Miss Potter had marched up to me, cleared her throat, and said, in her accented Gallacian, "Until next we meet, young sinner! If you die before me, we'll drink the country dry in your memory."

I bowed very deeply, wished her the best, then pulled Angus aside, and hissed, "You've *got* to get that phrase book away from her."

"I threw it out days ago," said Angus, sounding both proud and appalled. "She's got a terrifying memory."

In any event, I was the only one home when Father Sebastian rode into the stableyard. Bors trailed behind var, looking somewhat overawed.

"I've buried the poor soul you sent me," va announced, swinging down from var horse. "What was left of them, anyway."

"Then come and have some wine, both of you," I said. "We didn't have a funeral feast, but we can probably rustle something up."

Bread and cheese and leftover sausage was the best we could manage, but Father Sebastian had doubtless gotten far less from far more devout parishioners and did not complain.

"Any idea who she was?" I asked, pouring the wine. Bors astonished me by asking for a small glass, so I gave him a generous thimbleful.

Father Sebastian shook var head. "I consulted the parish records back for over a century," va said. "The Church gets very annoyed if you go burying the wrong people in consecrated ground. But even in a town as small as Wolf's Ear, and even with records as gossipy as ours, there are too many people who slip through the cracks."

I nodded. It didn't surprise me.

"If I had to guess . . ." The priest steepled var fingers. "About a hundred and forty years ago, a minor lord bought this lodge. The parish records a number of births among his servants—or former servants—with no father's name given."

"Ah." I set down the lump of bread and cheese. "That sort, was he."

Father Sebastian lifted var hands. "I've no proof, though the parish records are less than kind about him, I admit. He seems to have been less than welcome in the family seat, and stayed here most of the year."

Which was not proof, of course. The moroi's bones could have been older or much younger. Perhaps it didn't matter anyway. Like I said before, true stories rarely wrap up neatly.

"At any rate, I decided that on balance one should err on the side of mercy, and buried her in the churchyard. My superiors may send me nasty letters or not, as they choose."

"May we always have the choice to err on the side of mercy," I said, lifting my wine.

We finished our impromptu feast and Father Sebastian took var leave. The priest swung up on var horse and looked down at me from that height. "Interesting thing about that lord."

"Oh?"

"He died quite young. Of pneumonia." Father Sebastian gazed at me keenly, and I found that for once, I had nothing to say.

The priest nodded, perhaps satisfied, and turned var horse. "Young Bors here had something to ask you. I told him that you'd hear him out. God watch over you in your travels, Lieutenant Easton. Bors, I will see you Sunday."

The sound of hoofbeats faded away as I tried to work out time lines in my head. Had the lord been first? Had others followed, until she was dug up and reburied in the springhouse to keep her from walking? And then she'd slept for what . . . a century and change? Until time had stopped the water's flow, and then she'd found Codrin.

Hell, for all I knew she was responsible for the curious absence of mice, despite their nests.

I shook myself and turned to Bors, who was mutilating his hat in much the same fashion that I had mauled mine when speaking to Codrin's daughter. "What am I hearing out, Bors?" Angus had told me that he'd discreetly paid Bors his wages through the end of the year. Hopefully we'd be well away before the Widow found out.

He glanced toward the springhouse, then back to me. "Will you be leaving?"

"In a day or two, I think. I'm well enough to travel now." Truth was, I'd only been waiting because I hadn't wanted to cut Angus's time with Miss Potter short.

Bors nodded. After a moment he said, almost shyly, "If you need a caretaker while you're gone . . . I thought maybe I could

stay. I know my letters. I could write to you and tell you what
the lodge needs."

I stared at him.

"They won't be long letters," he said anxiously.

Bors could write letters like a frustrated Russian novelist
for all I cared. That wasn't the issue. "You want to stay *here*?
After everything?"

Bors looked around the hunting lodge, the grounds, the
stableyard. "It's not the place's fault," he said reasonably. "It
was here before she was. It doesn't deserve to fall apart because
something bad happened here." Another of his long silences,
and then he added, "Something bad happened to both of us,
too. We don't deserve to fall apart either."

"Bors," I said, when I could speak again, "you are going to
be a very wise man someday. The position is yours for as long
as you want it."

"Thank you, sir." And then, as close to sly as I've ever seen
Bors be, "Though I don't think Nana will come visit me often."

I burst out laughing, even though it hurt my chest, and Bors
joined me. The sounds of our laughter rang through the woods
and nothing reached out to silence the echoes. And if they have
not since died, so far as I know they are ringing there still.

ACKNOWLEDGMENTS

Here we are again at the end of another of Easton's adventures, and I am once again astounded by how many people's help goes into a book that somehow only has my name on the cover.

There's a truism that "all knowledge is contained in fandom," meaning that if you ask a question, some fan somewhere happens to have done their doctoral thesis on it, and it is terrifyingly true in the case of this book. I asked Twitter what kind of gun Alex would have, and people fell out of the woodwork to discuss the matter and send me helpful pointers. Thank you all very much for that—the two groups who will *always* spot the details are the gun people and the textile people, and while I fear the textile people somewhat more, I like to stay on the right side of both of them.

And speaking of someone doing their thesis, my greatest and most heartfelt thanks to Isabelle Avakumovic-Pointon, a reader who, as it turned out, was working on her master's in nineteenth-century Balkan history. Since I was writing a story about a person from a fictional country having flashbacks to a real country, while myself being from a different continent, her input was enormously helpful. Anything I got right is probably thanks to her careful reading and notes.

While Gallacia is a fictional place in the Ruritanian tradition, Alex's war is a very real one, the Serbian–Bulgarian War of 1885. Probably most wars are confusing for the people on the ground, but this particular one was even more baffling and badly run than most. I can't possibly do it justice in a paragraph, but it's worth reading about if you ever want an object lesson in how *not* to invade Bulgaria. (Please do not invade Bulgaria under any circumstances.)

Soldier's heart is also a very real condition, though these days we call it PTSD. Many thanks to my friend Shepherd for his insights and to the many, many brave people who have discussed their own PTSD in public and the complicated ways in which it can manifest.

The slimy earthtongue is a real mushroom, *Geoglossum difforme*, endangered due to habitat loss. (I mention this because the stinking redcap in *What Moves the Dead* isn't a real mushroom, and people asked.) The bleeding bonnet is also a real mushroom, though more widely spread than the poor slimy earthtongue.

Also . . . I'm not sure if this is *thanks*, so much as an honorable mention for the Finnish people in general and my buddy Heli in particular, who introduced me to homemade salmiakki liqueur. I realize it's only one line in the book, but that drink is stamped upon my very soul.

As for the matter of actually turning my blatherings in a Word doc into a real, coherent book, all credit to the awesome people at Tor Nightfire—my editor, Lindsey Hall, who understands what I'm trying to do and shows me how to do it; Kelly Lonesome; Aislyn Fredsall; and everybody else. And huge thanks to Christina Mrozik, whose covers grace these books and who I'm pretty well convinced made them as successful as they've been.

Thanks as well to my agent, Helen, who understands that my desire in life is to sit in a room writing books while someone slips checks under the door and does her best to make that happen.

And finally, as always, my thanks and my heart to my husband, Kevin, without whom I would still write books, but not nearly as many, since I would be trying to juggle all the things that he handles. Without him, I would live on frozen pizza, eaten over the sink so I didn't have to do dishes, and my primary social interaction would be talking to the Roomba. Whatever I did to deserve you, it wasn't enough.

T. Kingfisher
August 2023
Pittsboro, NC

ABOUT THE AUTHOR

T. Kingfisher is the adult fiction pseudonym of Ursula Vernon, the multi-award-winning author of *Digger* and *Dragonbreath*. She is an author and illustrator based in North Carolina who has been nominated for the Ursa Major Award, the Eisner Awards, and has won the Nebula Award for Best Short Story for "Jackalope Wives" in 2015 and the Hugo Award for Best Novelette for "The Tomato Thief" in 2017. Her debut adult horror novel, *The Twisted Ones*, won the 2020 Dragon Award for Best Horror Novel, and was followed by the critically acclaimed *The Hollow Places*.

THE HOLLOW PLACES
BY T. KINGFISHER

Kara finds the words in the mysterious bunker that she's discovered behind a hole in the wall of her uncle's house. Freshly divorced and living back at home, Kara now becomes obsessed with these cryptic words and starts exploring this peculiar area—only to discover that it holds portals to countless alternate realities. But these places are haunted by creatures that seem to hear thoughts…and the more one fears them, the stronger they become.

With her distinctive "delightfully fresh and subversive" (*SF Bluestocking*) prose and the strange, sinister wonder found in Guillermo del Toro's *Pan's Labyrinth*, *The Hollow Places* is another compelling and white-knuckled horror novel that you won't be able to put down.

"*The Hollow Places* is gripping, bold, sharply witty, inventive and most of all – terrifying! It's every bit as unmissable as *The Twisted Ones*. T. Kingfisher most definitely has a new fan!"
Alison Littlewood

For more fantastic fiction, author events,
exclusive excerpts, competitions, limited editions and more

VISIT OUR WEBSITE
titanbooks.com

LIKE US ON FACEBOOK
facebook.com/titanbooks

FOLLOW US ON TWITTER AND INSTAGRAM
@TitanBooks

EMAIL US
readerfeedback@titanemail.com